The
Invisible
Detective

The
Invisible
Detective

Killing Time

JUSTIN RICHARDS

POCKET
BOOKS

POCKET
BOOKS

First published in the UK in 2003 by Pocket Books
An imprint of Simon & Schuster UK Ltd.
Africa House, 64-78 Kingsway, London WC2B 6AH
A Viacom Company

A CIP catalogue record for this book is available from the British Library

ISBN 0 7434 6225 4

1 3 5 7 9 10 8 6 4 2

Printed and bound in Germany
by GGP Media GmbH

*For Stephen Cole – peerless editor, and
'godfather' to the Invisible Detective.*

COLLECT ALL THE
INVISIBLE DETECTIVE'S
AMAZING ADVENTURES!

THE PARANORMAL PUPPET SHOW
THE SHADOW BEAST
GHOST SOLDIERS

Coming soon
THE FACES OF EVIL
THE WEB OF ANUBIS

All Pocket Books are available by post from:
Simon & Schuster Cash Sales, PO Box 29
Douglas, Isle of Man IM99 1BQ
Credit cards accepted.
Please telephone 01624 836000
fax 01624 670923, Internet
http://www.bookpost.co.uk or email:
bookshop@enterprise.net for details

Chapter 1

'It was the watch that killed him.'

Jonny had tired of holding the fishing rod and it was now propped up in a corner behind the curtain. Together with Meg, he stood peering out through the narrow gap between the curtains, watching as Brandon Lake – the Invisible Detective – held his consulting session.

Of course, Jonny and Meg both knew who the Invisible Detective really was. Flinch knew too, but she was back at the disused warehouse that was their den on Cannon Street. Jonny, Meg and Flinch, together with Art, were the Cannoniers.

They were also the Invisible Detective. At least, Art was the Invisible Detective. It had been his idea, and he was the one sitting in the threadbare armchair, its high back turned to the audience in the dimly lit room above the locksmith's shop. Jonny could see Art's silhouette, huddled inside an enormous overcoat, one hand emerging to be glimpsed as part of the act as Art spoke.

The detective's voice was artificially deep. It

always sounded odd to Jonny, but then he knew it belonged to a fourteen-year-old boy pretending to be a man.

'You say the watch killed him?' the deep voice said.

The man who had been speaking shuffled uncomfortably. Jonny could see him against the light from the stairwell at the back of the room. 'He was fine till he got given that watch. Few years ago, it was. Since then he's not never been well.'

'A coincidence?'

The man carried on, seeming to ignore the suggestion. 'Funny thing is, his wife's been better than ever, and she were always the sickly one. My brother – he'd not had a day off ill in his life before she gave him that watch. Except after they'd had a row, but that's always the way.'

Meg gave a quiet snort beside Jonny. He was not sure if it was meant to be in agreement or not. 'Is he telling the truth?' Jonny whispered to her. She would know. Meg could tell if people were lying.

She nodded. 'As far as he knows what the truth is,' she whispered. 'But just because he thinks it's something to do with his brother's watch, that doesn't mean he's right.'

'Shall I tell Art?' Jonny glanced at the fishing rod. He had a stub of pencil and a few sheets of paper in his pocket. He could easily attach a note to the fishing hook and cast it across to Art without the audience seeing. It was the only way they had of passing messages.

But Meg shook her head. 'Don't bother. He knows.'

She was right. The truth was, Jonny decided, that he was bored. Usually he relished the weekly consulting sessions. But for the last few months very little of interest had come the Invisible Detective's way. And now they were being asked to believe a man had lost his good health and died because his wife gave him a watch. Was that a step up from last week's suggestion that the landlord of a pub in Cheapside was watering his beer? By chatting to the cellar boy, it had taken Art five minutes to discover that he wasn't. But he *was* selling a pale ale as best bitter to make an extra ha'penny a pint.

'And why, Mr Mason,' the detective was asking, 'do you believe so firmly that your brother's death was from anything other than natural causes? It seems to me that it would be difficult to prove otherwise if his doctor was convinced there was no foul play.'

'No foul play?' Mason took a step forwards, his hands bunched into fists at his side. 'I know what the doctors said. I know the post-mortem revealed nothing. But I saw him. I watched him go from a healthy man in his fifties to a wreck.'

Someone close to Mason muttered, though Jonny did not catch what they said, just the shape of the sound. Mason rounded on them. 'Weren't drink, neither,' he shouted. 'He never touched a drop. But I know this – when he died, you'd've thought he was in his eighties, not his fifties. He was all shrivelled up, like a prune. Wasted away, he did. Heart attack?' Mason was shaking his head. 'He died of old age.'

There was silence after his outburst. Jonny wondered how Art would deal with this. What would the Invisible Detective say?

'I appreciate the strength of your feelings,' the detective said at last. 'And of course I shall give your concerns my most serious consideration. But I have to tell you that if the doctors believe your brother's death was due to natural causes, then that is indeed the most likely explanation.'

Jonny waited for Mason to start shouting again. But he did not. He nodded slowly, as if considering, and when he spoke his voice was quieter and calmer. 'Well, I suppose that's all I can ask, sir. Maybe you're right. Maybe they're all right. But it don't seem . . . natural. He never liked that watch. Said it didn't keep the time. Kept it in a drawer and forgot about it, I dare say. Till right at the end.'

'And when did he receive this pocket watch?'

Mason coughed and shuffled his feet. 'Well, about 1920,' he admitted. There was some laughter at this, though Mason ignored it, adding loudly, 'But he was about thirty then, and died of old age less than twenty years after.'

'Perhaps,' the Invisible Detective said, 'you could leave the pocket watch for my examination.'

'Yeah. I'll do that.' Mason was already turning to go. 'You can keep it. Do instead of a sixpence, I expect.'

* * *

When everyone had left, Jonny counted the money. Anyone who asked the Invisible Detective a question left sixpence on a plate at the back of the room.

Meg helped Art out of the huge coat, and they all paused as they heard the sound of rapid footsteps on the stairs.

'Hello, Flinch,' Art called out. He was grinning, flicking his dark hair away from his forehead. 'Thanks, Meg,' he added quietly as she took the coat from him.

Meg was almost as tall as Art – and almost as old. Now that the curtains were open, the light was shining in from the street outside – harsh streetlights softened by the distance and the dust on the windows. It made Meg's mass of red curls seem almost to glow.

Meg was not smiling, but that did not surprise Jonny – Meg rarely smiled. Flinch, by contrast, was grinning broadly as she reached the top of the stairs. She was the smallest of the Cannoniers, and the youngest, though she had lived on the streets for so long she had no idea how old she really was. Her long fair hair was matted and grimy, her face smudged with dirt. But despite her lack of a home or family, Flinch was almost always smiling. The Cannoniers were her family. Their den was her home.

'Two shillings and a pocket watch,' Jonny announced.

'Is that all?' Meg demanded.

'Better than last week,' Jonny told her.

'But still not enough to pay Mr Jerrickson the rent we owe for this room,' Art pointed out.

'We could sell the watch,' Flinch suggested. She reached out to take it from Jonny. 'Or pawn it. I've never had a watch.'

'Perhaps you should have it, then,' Art suggested.

Flinch turned the watch over in her hands, then dangled it by its chain, letting it swing back and forth. 'Don't need a watch,' she said. 'Nowhere to keep it.'

'You attach it to your waistcoat button and keep it in the pocket,' Jonny told her. 'That's why it's called a pocket watch.'

Flinch still seemed unimpressed. 'Wouldn't mind a waistcoat. Keep me warm.'

As if to make the point, she huddled inside her thin coat and folded her arms about herself.

The cuffs came down over her hands, the coat was so big. It had been Meg's, and while it was wearing thin and was really meant to keep out a summer breeze rather than the chill of the February air, it was the best the Cannoniers had found for her.

'We need to be making more money,' Meg said. 'Then we can pay the rent, and get Flinch a new coat.'

'*Waist*coat. For my watch.' She took the watch back from Jonny and re-examined it. 'If we can make it go.'

'We need a case,' Jonny decided. 'A proper case, not some haunted watch.'

'Haunted?' Flinch hurriedly gave it back to him. 'Doesn't work anyway.'

'Probably needs winding up,' Art said gently. 'But first things first.'

'You mean paying the rent?' Meg asked.

'I'll talk to Mr Jerrickson tomorrow. But by "first things first" I meant, let's get back to the den.' He grinned at Flinch. 'Jonny can tell you all about the Case of the Haunted Watch, and I've got some biscuits.'

Flinch's smile grew even wider at this and she skipped after Art to the stairs.

Meg followed and Jonny came last, slipping the two shillings into his trouser pocket for now. He spared a moment to look at the watch before he stuffed that into his pocket too.

It was a funny thing, he thought, as he made his way down the stairs. Flinch was right – the hands of the watch were not moving. Even the second hand was halted between the six and the seven. But as he had looked at the watch, just before he put it in his pocket, he was sure he had heard it ticking.

Arthur Drake had seen the clock in the antiques shop before, but he did not recall noticing the inscription. Across the middle of the face of the grandfather clock, it said 'Tempus non fugit'. The stylised writing looked the same as on a clock that Arthur had recently found – except that *his* clock said 'Edax Rerum'. Arthur had come across the expression *Tempus fugit*, but not *Tempus non fugit*. There again, this clock was stopped, so perhaps the variation was appropriate.

The old brass carriage clock that Arthur had discovered in a deserted house was just one of the weird things he had come across recently. Several of them – the most strange – he had found in this very shop.

There was the casebook of the Invisible Detective, which seemed to be written in his own handwriting and had been kept by a boy called Art Drake – a boy whom Arthur now knew to be his own grandfather.

There was a large multicoloured pebble which had such depths when you looked into it that Arthur could see the past, could remember what had happened to the Invisible Detective, to Art and the Cannoniers, as if he had been there. Except the memories sometimes slipped away, like a dream. He could read the casebook too, although its words seemed to fade from his memory so he could not remember what he had just read. It was as if, he had decided, he could only hold on to the memories when the time was *right*.

And there was the clock. He had found it in a deserted house where Art and the Cannoniers had solved one of their mysteries – where they had encountered the Ghost Soldiers, as the casebook called them. Also in the house, Arthur had found Sarah Bustle.

Sarah went to the same school as Arthur, though she was older and in the next year. Arthur had only recently discovered that his dad knew Sarah's mum, and that Sarah somehow knew about the Invisible Detective. But although they exchanged a few words during break or after school, there had been no real opportunity to discuss what each of them knew or how they came to know it.

That was about to change, which was why Arthur had come to the little antiques shop on Cannon Street that he passed every day on his way to and from school.

They had told Arthur at the home that his grandfather had taken a taxi to go and visit a friend. It had not taken Arthur long to guess who the friend might be. The only local person, apart from himself and his dad, that Grandad knew was the owner of the antiques shop. Sure enough, he had found the two old men sitting at the back of the dusty shop, drinking tea and talking quietly.

At first they were so still and quiet that Arthur had not seen them. Among the bric-à-brac and odds and ends they seemed just like two more dusty antiques. But Arthur did not tell them that.

'So when do you leave?' Grandad asked.

'Half-term is all next week. So we can pack after school on Friday and Dad wants to make an early start on Saturday morning. It's a long way to Cornwall.'

Grandad nodded. 'It is. There'll be lots of traffic too, if it's the start of half-term. Not so much as in the summer, but still busy.'

'Where are you staying?' the old shopkeeper asked. His wispy grey hair seemed to shimmer as he spoke. His eyes were distorted by thick spectacles.

'Some village.' Arthur shrugged. 'Dad's hired a cottage for the week. It's quite big apparently, that's why he told her mum that Sarah could come with us. And he's got some report he has to write, so he wants time to himself.'

'Sarah?' Grandad asked, his eyes shining in a sudden ray of sunlight that filtered through the dusty windows.

'Sarah Bustle. From school.' Arthur shuffled, embarrassed. 'Her mum is a friend of Dad's,' he explained quickly. 'Only she's off on some business trip to America. Sarah was going to her father's, but

Dad said she could come with us. So I have some company while he's working.'

'Bustle,' Grandad repeated quietly. 'Rings a bell.'

'She's got an annoying little brother. But he's not coming, luckily. Going to stay with some other friend and cause trouble there, I expect. He never stops talking. Just goes on and on. Never knows when to stop.'

'Really?' Grandad seemed amused at this. 'Well, it will be nice for you to have someone about your own age to spend time with. Come and see me when you get back, and tell me all about it.'

Arthur shrugged again. 'All right. I expect it'll be dead boring, though. Some little fishing village where nothing ever happens.'

He was turning to go, having said goodbye to Grandad and the shopkeeper, when the clock struck. Arthur had not heard it strike before. He had thought it was broken, but perhaps that was just the hands. That was when he noticed the script on the dial.

And it was then that it occurred to him that although he had mentioned the clock he'd found to Sarah, she had never seen it. He decided he would take it with him to Cornwall, if only to give them

13

something to talk about – a way of starting discussions and finding out what she really knew about the Invisible Detective. And, in a way, that was when the adventure began.

Chapter 2

The warehouse was on the corner of Cannon Street and it had not been used for years – at least, not as a warehouse. But it was used now, by the Cannoniers as their den. Once huge lengths of carpet had been stored there, having been shipped in from all over the world and on their way to line the floors of hotels, country houses and even palaces. Or so Flinch liked to think.

The last carpets were still there. Enormous long rolls. But the thick woollen pile had faded and compacted until it was almost reduced to the bare threads and canvas backing. A layer of dust coated everything, except where it had been exorcised by the children's playing or sitting or, in Flinch's case, sleeping. She had a sort of nest made from the better ends of carpet and a few blankets. An old cushion for which Jonny's mum had once made a cover served as a pillow – the cover all but worn through. Mice had eaten away at the stuffing, but it was comfortable and Flinch liked to think she could smell the hint of Jonny's home on it.

Jonny was acting the fool now, and Meg was watching with apparent disapproval. But Flinch thought it was funny and she could see that Meg's mouth was twitching the way it did when she was trying not to smile. She looked so much older when she was being serious.

Jonny was pretending to try to lift one of the rolls of carpet. Of course, there was no way he could manage – the four of them had barely been able to shift one of the heavy rolls across the floor to arrange a seating area. But Jonny was being a workman from the days when the warehouse was still in use. Part of the time he was miming moving the carpet, part of the time he was waving directions to imaginary colleagues.

Art was sitting alone on one of the rolled carpets. He was staring off into space with his 'thinking' face on. The pocket watch was dangling on its chain from his index finger, swinging gently as he continued to think.

There was a sudden splutter from beside Flinch as Meg tried to stifle a sudden laugh. In his efforts to manipulate the carpet, Jonny had tumbled head over heels and his feet were now visible, waving pathetically above the rolls. Flinch giggled helplessly as Jonny's legs disappeared and his peeved face rose into view.

'That wasn't funny,' he complained.

Now Meg did laugh. Her face shone with amusement, and Flinch found she was clutching the older girl as they both rocked with amusement.

The sound had shocked Art out of his thoughts. He stared across at Jonny, who was now laughing too, then sprang to his feet. He shuffled past Meg and Flinch, dropping the pocket watch into Flinch's lap as he went.

'Not like that, Mr Levin,' Art called out in a broad cockney accent. 'Do yerself a mischief, you will. This is how you do it.' So saying, he mimicked Jonny's previous accident and tumbled headlong over the carpet just as Jonny had.

'You see the problem now, don't you, Mr Drake?'

Jonny's accent was not as good, but Flinch clapped with delight, and Meg had given up pretending she found the game silly.

The two boys were working together now, pretending to try to lift the carpet. Art had called over more imaginary workers and was leaping from one side of the carpet to the other, changing his voice as he was one person after another.

'Reckon it's too heavy, mate.'

'Bring it up your side a bit, chum.'

'What about trying to roll it?'

'Not this way – that's my foot.'

Jonny was doing his best to keep up, but he was fighting a losing battle and had almost collapsed with the effort of trying not to laugh.

As she watched their antics, Flinch was holding the pocket watch. There was a brass ring where the thin chain was attached at the top of the watch, and within this was a winding stud. It was a small round knob, milled so it could be gripped easily between the thumb and forefinger. Without really realising what she was doing, Flinch was twisting it, rolling it one way and then the other. But Art and Jonny held her full attention and she did not notice what was happening to the watch.

A walkway ran round the top of the huge room they were in. They never went up there – the stairs had almost completely rotted away and they knew from experience that they were treacherous. Outside the stained upper-floor windows, level with the walkway, there was a streetlight. Its pale glow shone down through the dust that was swirling in the air in front of Flinch and Meg. It made the flecks sparkle as they twisted and fell. It seemed to Flinch, as she watched Art and Jonny, that the haze of dust was getting thicker, that the particles were somehow joining together. That the air itself was becoming solid . . .

And suddenly, there they were – people. Meg gave a gasp of surprise and Flinch screwed her eyes tight shut. But only for a moment, then she was peeping out between her fingers.

Jonny and Art were still clowning around with the carpet, pretending to lift it. But Flinch could see the amazement on their faces too, as the carpet did indeed lift into the air. There were people, men in old-fashioned clothes. They wore no jackets and their sleeves were rolled up as several of them hefted the carpet and started to walk with it towards the double doors at the end of the warehouse.

'Careful with that,' someone called – his voice a faint but clear echo. 'That one's for the Duke of Devonshire.'

'And he don't mean the public house on Degard Street,' another voice called in a strange half-echo.

There was laughter. Several of the faint men

carrying the carpet glanced back. One of them was looking straight at Flinch, but he seemed not to notice her.

She turned to see where the man was looking. Behind her stood a portly figure in a long dark jacket. He was holding a cigar, but he seemed as faint and indistinct as the smoke that rose from it and twisted like dust in the air between them. He smiled. And as he smiled, he seemed to return to dust and drift away.

When Flinch turned back, the warehouse was quiet and empty again, except for herself and Meg sitting side by side on an ancient roll of carpet, and Art and Jonny standing a few yards away, their mouths hanging open in amazement.

Meg's voice was a harsh whisper that broke the near-silence. 'Look,' she said. 'Look at the watch.'

It was lying in Flinch's lap, where she had dropped it when she covered her eyes. The hands were moving now. Not steadily, as you would expect of a watch, but rapidly, almost frantically. And they were moving backwards.

Flinch leapt to her feet in surprise. The watch slipped from her lap and clattered to the floor, spinning at her feet. When it stopped, she bent slowly to pick it up. But she could see before her fingers reached it that the hands of the watch were still once more. Somewhere, perhaps in the back of her mind, Flinch thought she could hear the fading sound of laughter.

Being February it was cold. The breeze was bitter, cutting through Arthur's coat and making his ears sting. But it was a bright, sunny day and the salt smell of the sea was refreshing.

Dad had sent them to explore the beach while he got the heating working and unpacked the food and supplies they had brought with them. Arthur was glad of the chance to talk to Sarah. She had insisted he go in the front of the car with his dad, so they had not been able to talk on the long journey down to Porthellis.

The cottage was on the cliffs, exposed to the wind and isolated. It overlooked the sea to the north and the church to the west. The village of Porthellis was below the church, clustered round a small bay. A jetty thrust out into the bay and the main industry still seemed to be fishing. Beyond the village, on the opposite 'arm' of the bay from the cottage, was the lighthouse.

According to one of the brochures left out in the cottage, the lighthouse was now a museum of some sort. There was a whole stack of leaflets on the table inside the door, but from a quick look Porthellis Lighthouse Museum was the only attraction anywhere closer than St Ives.

'Might be worth a look,' Arthur had said, waving the leaflet at Sarah and his dad and hoping he did not sound too bored.

Sarah and Arthur had decided to leave walking to the village until later. For now they had taken the steep path down the cliffs to the narrow stretch of beach immediately below the cottage. It was hard work negotiating the path, and Arthur was not looking forward to climbing back up again. Perhaps they could walk round to the little harbour they had driven past on the way and reach the village from the beach.

'So what do you know about the Invisible Detective?' Arthur asked as soon as he had got his breath back. He didn't see any point in waiting to ask. 'The *real* Invisible Detective, not your website.'

Sarah was drawing in the damp sand with the toe of her boot, making long undulating lines. The letter 'S', Arthur realised. She did not answer for a while, and he wondered if she was ever going to.

'Not a lot really,' she said at last. 'Not like you. What do you know about it?'

That threw Arthur slightly. 'Me?' He had not been expecting to get the question back. 'Well . . . lots, I suppose.'

'Good.' She traced out another lazy S in the sand. 'My dad told me stuff, but that was ages ago. It seemed like a good idea for a website. And he mentioned the house, of course.'

'Of course.' She must mean the derelict house where he had found the clock, where Sarah some-times went to get away from her noisy brother and do her homework. 'I've got his casebook. Art's, I mean.'

'Really?' She seemed impressed. 'Can I see it?'

Arthur wasn't sure about that. The book was somehow so personal – a link between himself and Art, his grandad. 'I . . . Some time, yes,' he decided. 'But I haven't brought it with me.'

'Oh.' She scuffed out several Ss with her heel. 'Never mind.'

'I brought the clock,' he offered. 'Remember, I told you I found a clock?'

But she did not seem to be listening. She was staring across the beach, towards a point where the cliffs swung round and provided some shelter. 'Who's that?' she asked.

It took Arthur a moment to see who she meant. The man was so still, he seemed to be part of the cliff. Frozen in time. It was only when he moved, leaning across to recharge his paintbrush, that Arthur saw him.

The artist was sitting on a folding wooden chair with a canvas seat and back, his easel angled so he could look out to sea and paint, presumably, what he saw. Sarah was already walking across the beach towards him. Arthur followed. As the sand got drier, the walking was more difficult. He could feel it shifting under his feet.

The man smiled at them as they approached, raising his paintbrush in greeting. The blue paint on the end of it was the only bright colour in sight, Arthur noted. The man was wearing a dull brown coat and he was sitting in front of the dull brown cliffs. Even the sand around him seemed dull brown.

His face was as weather-beaten and lined as the cliffs, as well as being the same colour. His eyes were dark, and the lower part of his face was smothered with a grisly, grey stubbly beard that looked like the dead grass at the end of the path Sarah and Arthur had taken down from the cottage.

'Afternoon,' the painter said as they reached him. Perhaps he had spoken before, but if he had his words had been whipped away by the breeze.

'Do you mind if we look?' Sarah asked, pointing to his easel.

'Go ahead.' He leaned back and let them see what he had been painting.

It was a ship caught in a storm. An old sailing ship, the mast broken and the sails falling. The sky was lit by stabs of lightning and the sea was a raging frenzy. Arthur glanced out to sea, comparing the calm ocean with what was in the painting. There was a similarity, he had to admit. He could tell it was the same stretch of sea. There were edges of the beach, of the cliffs and of the headland on the other side of the harbour that were hinted at on the extremes of the picture. The shipwreck was happening here, in front of him, except he could not see it.

'That's very good,' he said, though as soon as

25

he said it he felt embarrassed. Like he'd tell the man if the painting was rubbish.

But the artist smiled. 'Thank you, young man.'

'Arthur.'

'Thank you, Arthur.'

'I'm Sarah,' Sarah told him. 'And Arthur's right. It's terrific. Do you paint a lot?'

'All the time.'

'What sorts of things?' Arthur wondered.

'More often than not it's ships, the sea.' He put down the paintbrush, balancing it carefully on the palette that rested on a small table beside his chair. 'I have a little gallery in the village. Martin Sladden.' He reached across to shake their hands and Arthur caught the smell of oil paint as he gripped the man's dry, sandpaper hand.

'I know you can't see the ship or the storm out there,' he said as they continued to examine his painting. He tapped his forehead with a stained finger. 'But it's clear as day in here. I like to get things right, exactly right. Like the shape of the headland and the slope of the beach. The breakers and the foam. You have to be accurate, you know. Otherwise . . .' He sighed and picked up his brush again. 'Otherwise it's all a lie.'

There was a small boat out in the sea now, one of the fishing boats returning to the harbour. The sound of its engine was like the faint noise of an old lawnmower.

'Bob Saunders has had a good day, by the look of it,' Sladden said. 'He wouldn't be back this early unless his lobster pots were all full. You'll find him in the Smuggler's Rest this afternoon, I can tell you.'

'Is that the pub?' Sarah asked.

Sladden nodded. 'It's not bad,' he admitted. 'You'll find me there too, now and again.' He smiled and winked. 'On occasion.'

'Do you ever go out in the boats?' Arthur wondered. He quite fancied a trip out in a fishing boat and maybe Sladden could organise it.

But the man's smile disappeared at the question. 'No,' he said, suddenly absorbed once more in his work. He paused as he filled out a wave that was breaking over the side of the battered ship. 'I can look at it, paint it, even remember the way the damp gets everywhere on a ship. But no. Never. I never go to sea. Not any more.'

They watched him for a few minutes longer, but he was absorbed again in his work.

'Bye then,' Sarah said after a while. They waited

27

for a reply, but the painter just nodded and dabbed at the canvas.

They left him alone by the cliff and made their way back up the path to the cottage.

Chapter 3

Art took Flinch with him the next afternoon. Jonny was helping his dad with his accounts and Meg had gone home to spend time with her mother before her father came in from work. If he did.

Mr Jerrickson greeted the two of them with a smile. He was a short man with wispy grey hair that had thinned almost to nothing. 'Just the two of you today, is it?' he asked in a cracked voice. 'And how is Mr Lake keeping? I still hope he will be good enough to pay me a visit himself one day, you know.' The old man watched Art and Flinch through eyes that were enlarged by round, wire-rimmed pebble glasses.

'It's about the rent,' Art explained, once he had apologised that Brandon Lake could not come himself.

Mr Jerrickson nodded knowingly. 'Need another week, do you?'

'We have some money.' Art handed him several coins. 'We won't get any further behind, I promise.'

The old man counted the coins slowly from one wrinkled hand to the other. 'That's all right, my friend. It all helps, and it's not like I need the room for anything else.'

Art swallowed. Mr Jerrickson was always so good about the rent. He charged them next to nothing and he never complained when they were late. But that just made Art feel worse about it. If the old man had shouted, told them off, then Art would feel less guilty. But he was always quiet and kind and understanding.

'We got a watch,' Flinch said.

'Have you now?' The old man's faded eyes twinkled behind the lenses. 'Not sure that I need a watch. But I'll take a look at it if you like.'

'Doesn't work, though,' Flinch said as she handed it to him. She looked as if she was going to tell him more about it – maybe about the ghosts and how the hands had spun backwards – but Art nudged her and she bit her lip.

The locksmith turned the watch over, examining it carefully. 'Used to have something engraved on the back, I see.'

'It's the name of the previous owner,' Art explained. 'Neville Mason. It's all right, we were given it by his brother.'

'You've got better eyes than me,' Mr

Jerrickson said, peering closely at the back of the watch. 'Can't make out the letters it's so faded.'

'Faded?' Flinch leaned closer to look, making the old man move with surprise as her head almost touched his. But Flinch did not notice. 'Look, Art,' she said. 'It's nearly gone. It wasn't like that before.'

Art took the watch back from Mr Jerrickson. She was right, the name on the back had all but disappeared. Yet the previous day it had been clear enough to read easily. That was odd. First the ghosts – the sight of people from the past. Now this . . .

'*Tempus fugit*,' the old man said quietly.

'What's that?' Flinch asked.

'It's Latin. It means "Time flies".' He nodded at the watch. 'Written on the front, on the dial.'

'So it is,' Art said, turning the watch back over. That at least had not faded.

'Thank you for the offer,' Mr Jerrickson went on. 'But, as I say, I don't really need a watch.' He smiled, his face wrinkling more than usual with the movement. 'Especially a broken one. Now, if you had a nice antique grandfather clock, to go in the corner over there . . .'

31

'We'll find one,' Flinch promised.

'You let me know if you do, Miss Flinch.'

Flinch giggled at this, and grinned at Art.

Mr Jerrickson was amused too. He pulled something from his jacket pocket and handed it to Flinch. 'My card, Miss Flinch. You let me know if ever you need a lock opening or mending.'

Flinch stared at the card in surprise and awe. 'What does it say?' she asked.

The old man pointed a shaking finger at the printed words. 'That's my name, that's the name of the shop and that's the address.' He turned to Art. 'Take as long as you need for the rent.'

'Thanks.'

'And you might try the pawn shop on Abchurch Lane. Young Creighton knows a bit about watches, he might be interested. Tell him I sent you.'

Flinch was still clutching Mr Jerrickson's card when they found the pawn shop, tracing her finger across the printed words. Art was not hopeful. He could not imagine anyone would advance them much money for a broken watch, even if he could convince them it was somehow haunted. But it was worth a try, and it would be impolite not to take the old man's advice, having accepted his offer to delay paying the rent.

He was more hopeful as he looked round the shop. There were several clocks, with labels hanging from them, arranged on shelves. A display case on the side of the front desk was full of pocket watches. Again, they were all labelled and numbered for the day when they might be reclaimed.

'Young Creighton', if it was indeed him, looked to be in his sixties at least, with grey hair that was oiled across his scalp. Some of the oil seemed to have dripped down onto his stiff white collar.

'Mr Jerrickson is an old friend,' he wheezed, his voice throaty and hoarse. The butt end of a cigarette was burning out in an ashtray piled with other stubs, so Art could guess why he spoke like that. 'Let's have a look at it.' He picked up a jeweller's glass and pushed it into his eye, ready to inspect the merchandise.

Art handed him the watch. Creighton took it carefully and peered through the glass at the dial. Almost immediately, the glass fell from his eye, landing with a clatter on the counter between them. The man thrust the watch back at Art, who was surprised to see that his face was drawn and pale.

'Is this a joke?' the man hissed. 'What are you trying to do to me?' His hand was shaking and Art took the watch before he dropped it.

'I'm sorry,' Art stammered. 'What did we do?' He looked at Flinch, who had put Jerrickson's card away at last and seemed as surprised and confused as he was. 'If you're not interested, we can always try somewhere else . . .'

'Somewhere else?' The man seemed to have recovered slightly. But he was still shaking with emotion. 'You won't find anywhere that will give you a price for *that* watch, I can tell you. Except perhaps . . .' He shook his head and waved for them to leave. 'I'm sorry, I have things to do.'

'Like what?' Flinch asked, looking round.

'Things,' Creighton repeated forcefully.

'But what do we do with this?' Art held up the watch and was intrigued, though not now surprised, to see how the man seemed to shrink back at the sight of it.

'Destroy it,' he hissed. 'Throw it in the Thames.'

'You said "Except",' Art said slowly. 'Except where? Where could we get a price for it?' A few minutes earlier he would happily have thrown the thing in the river, but now he was determined to find out what was going on – why was the man so frightened?

'You could take it back to the watchmaker. He might have a use for it, but no one else will.'

'*Tempus fugit*?'

Creighton frowned. 'Edax Rerum,' he said. As soon as he had spoken, he caught his breath, as if regretting it. 'But I would keep well away from that place.' He turned away from them and busied himself rearranging bits and pieces on the shelves behind the counter. 'Throw it in the river,' he said without looking back. 'Get rid of it while you still have time.'

It looked to Meg as if the shop had been there for ever. It was the only premises on the street that was not boarded up. Even so, it seemed to have been deserted for years. The windows were so dirty it was almost impossible to see through them and the sign above the shop had faded to the point where it was almost illegible. Almost: 'Edax

Rerum' it said, in what remained of yellow or possibly gold lettering. The script was the same style as the '*Tempus fugit*' on the front of the watch.

It was hardly surprising, Meg thought, that the four of them were the only people within sight. As well as the fact that there was no reason for anyone to come here with the shops all gone, the smell of the river was distinctly unpleasant.

'Let's just leave it,' she said. 'There's nothing here.'

'I'm not sure,' Art said in a tone that suggested to Meg they might be here for a while yet. He was intrigued, fascinated . . . One thing Meg had learned about Art was that he would never willingly leave a mystery.

'It's listed in the telephone book, so it must have been open recently,' Jonny said.

'Then let's come back when it *is* open.'

'I don't think it will be,' Flinch said. 'I think it's all closed up now.'

Meg shrugged. 'That's it, then. Let's just leave it.'

'We could have a look round the back,' Art suggested brightly.

As soon as she saw the window, Meg sighed. She knew what would happen now. Sure enough, despite her telling them that they were not in the business of breaking into shops, even Jonny agreed with Art that they should 'have a quick look round, just to check everything's all right'. Despite herself, Meg realised she wanted to know what they would find as Art lifted Flinch up on his shoulders to the half-open window.

It was a narrow opening, but as ever Flinch somehow managed to squeeze herself through. She wriggled her way into the gap, her shoulders dislocating with an audible click that made Meg cringe. Then the little girl was gone, and the rest of them trooped back round to the front of the shop.

Flinch was grinning when she opened the door and let them in. Meg made to scowl back at her, but found that she was actually smiling. After all, she told herself, this could be the start of another adventure.

'It's all right,' Flinch said to Meg as they followed the boys inside. 'There's no one here.'

The dust was chokingly thick. It lay like a carpet across the floor and surfaces. The only marks were Flinch's footprints coming to the front door and Art's and Jonny's going back. Even the pictures hanging on the walls were coated with a layer of dust that made everything seem grey, like an old photograph.

There were clocks everywhere, though none of them seemed to be going. Grandfather clocks stood to attention in the corners of the room and along the back wall. There were carriage clocks of every shape, size and design on shelves. There was even a carved elephant standing beside the shop counter that had a clock set into its side. When Jonny wiped his hand across the counter, Meg could see through its murky glass top that it was filled with pocket watches laid out in lines on a faded velvet shelf inside.

'Here's the owner. Look.'

Flinch's voice startled Meg. She thought for a second that Flinch meant the owner had arrived, and she felt the bottom of her stomach fall away in trepidation. But Flinch was pointing at a framed photograph on the wall.

Jonny wiped the photograph with the side of his already dusty hand. It was a picture of the shop, almost exactly as it was now, but without the dirt and grime. A man was standing proudly behind the counter, his arms open as if welcoming the photographer into his shop. The man was completely bald, his face smooth. He had a thin moustache that was two straight lines across his pale face separated by a small gap under his nose – like the hands of a clock.

While Meg, Jonny and Flinch looked at the photograph, Art was opening a drawer at the bottom of the counter. He lifted out a large leather-bound book.

'What's that?' Jonny asked. 'Looks like a ledger.'

'We shouldn't just go through his things,' Meg pointed out.

But Art had already opened the book. 'Sales ledger. You're right, Jonny.' He leafed carefully through the brittle pages. 'Goes right back to the 1840s. Look. And the last entry is . . .' He turned to the back of the book and then back through several blank pages. '1921.'

'That's sixteen years ago,' Meg pointed out.

'Maybe it's an old book?' Jonny said. 'Perhaps he takes the current ledger home when the shop's shut.' He knelt down to rummage in the drawer where the ledger had been.

'This shop has not been open recently,' Meg insisted. 'No one's been here but us. Look at the footprints in the dust. There are only ours.'

Art had his casebook out and was copying down the last few entries from the ledger. 'Might be worth seeing if any of these people are still about,' he said. 'Funny thing, there's that sale in 1921 – to Mrs Mason, of course. *Two* pocket watches, in fact. But before that there's nothing since 1892.'

'Not likely they'll be around then.' Meg told him.

'The clocks might be.'

'Look at this.' Jonny was holding another book, smaller than the ledger, more like a school exercise book. 'It looks like a balance sheet,' he said, flicking through the pages. 'It lists pairs of clocks and watches.'

'All the sales are in pairs,' Art said, turning back through the ledger. 'Perhaps that's how he makes them.'

Further discussion was halted by the sound of a clock chiming. It was a sudden, unexpected and melancholy sound that startled Meg. She was pleased to see that Art and Jonny both jumped as well.

'Flinch!' Art said with a nervous laugh. 'You frightened us.'

'Sorry.' She looked sheepish. Her hand was still at the clock face. It was an old wooden clock mounted on the wall beside the photograph of the shopkeeper. 'I just wondered if it still worked.' The clock was now ticking noisily. It gave the time as almost quarter past nine.

'Come on,' said Art, closing the ledger. A puff of dust rose from the pages as they snapped shut. He replaced it in the drawer, taking the smaller book from Jonny and putting that away as well. 'Meg's right, we shouldn't really poke about in the clockmaker's private stuff.'

'Are we going to visit the people who bought his clocks?' Flinch wanted to know as they left.

'I think it's worth it,' Art said. 'Just so we know that there's nothing really odd going on and the Invisible Detective can put Mr Mason's mind at rest about his brother.'

Meg was the last to leave. She pulled the door closed behind her, glancing back round the room as she did so. Apart from the marks in the dust, nobody would know they had been there. That and the fact that Flinch had started that clock going.

She paused, halfway across the street. Flinch was skipping ahead with Art, and Jonny was sauntering behind them, his hands in his pockets. The clock, Meg realised – when she had looked back into the room, she was certain it had said ten past nine. Yet she was almost sure it had been at quarter past when Flinch set it going. She turned back towards the shop, staring at its faded paintwork and grimy windows. And gasped.

For a moment, just the briefest instant, she was certain someone was watching her – looking back out through the window by the door. A trick of the light, she told herself. The sun reflecting on the dust, or a glimpse of one of the clocks inside. Making it look as if a pale, round face with a thin, straight moustache was watching them as they left.

She turned and ran after her friends.

At the top of the path, Arthur paused to get his breath back. But Sarah did not seem to need a rest.

The wind was blowing her long black hair around her face as she strode out along the path that ran parallel to the cliff edge.

'Shouldn't we get back to the cottage?' Arthur wondered as he caught her up.

'There's ages yet.' She did not turn round or slacken her pace. 'Besides, I want to look at the church.'

'Why?'

'I don't know. Because it's there, I suppose. It might be interesting.'

There was a gate into the churchyard, but the church itself was locked. It was a small stone structure, odd in that the tower was a short distance from the main building. The tower had its own door and that too was locked.

There was a narrow path that ran round the churchyard, weaving in and out of the graves. One corner of the churchyard was given over to trees, so it seemed as if a small wood had wandered in and taken over. The graves ran right up to the edge of the trees, but then stopped.

Despite the bright sunlight, it was dark in among the trees. Arthur could make out nothing except the black ribbon of the path as it wound through. He hesitated at the edge, but Sarah walked on into the wood without pausing.

'You coming?' she called back over her shoulder.

Arthur hurried after her. 'Might as well. I wonder how old the church is.'

She shrugged. 'Looks medieval. Most of them are.'

Did she know that or was she guessing? Arthur wondered. Medieval could mean anything. 'And why's the tower so far from the church?'

She did not answer that one.

The way the light was filtered through the trees made it look like the ground was covered with golden leaves. But that was just an illusion, just the dappling of the sun on the ground.

The dark trunks seemed to close in around them as they made their way through the shadows. Then Arthur noticed that one of the tree trunks close to the edge of the little wood was not dark. It was white. And it was shaped like a signpost. Intrigued, he stepped off the path on to the soft grassy ground and went over to it.

'Hey – look at this.'

'What is it?' Sarah asked. She did not sound terribly interested.

'I think it's some sort of monument.'

Now that he was closer to it, Arthur could see that what he had thought was a tree was actually a stone upright and what he had taken for branches were the crumbling remains of the arms of a cross. At the base of the stone cross crouched two angels, facing outwards. One had lost its head and its wings were chipped. The other still had a head, but the features of the face had all but weathered away, so that it seemed to be wearing a pale, blank mask.

Between the angels were the crumbling, broken remains of a stone slab. Moss and lichen were growing over it now, but Arthur could just make out where there were names carved underneath them. Across the top, the lettering was larger and deeper and easier to read.

'We commend them to the deep,' Arthur read out. 'The brave sailors and captain of the *Kairos*. Lost on these shores, 19 February 1843. This is their last haven.'

'They must be buried here,' Sarah said. She knelt in front of the slab and brushed away some of the moss with her hand. 'Seven sailors. Look.'

Arthur could see the names more clearly now. 'Captain James Graves' was at the top of the list, his name slightly larger than the others. He read them aloud: 'Michael Birmingham, Heywood Fairling, Neville Broadwell, William Feather.' He knelt down beside Sarah, tracing his finger along the letters of the last but one name. 'Is that Luke Feather? His brother perhaps. I can't make out this last one.'

'It used to say Pieter Schneider. But now, alas, it has crumbled away.'

Arthur had not heard the man approaching, and, from her startled reaction, neither had Sarah. They both stood up abruptly, turning to face him. He was just a dark silhouette, a sliver of sunlight picking out a clerical collar as he took a step towards them and extended a dark arm. It took Arthur a while to realise he was offering to shake hands.

'Is this your church?' Sarah asked.

'I suppose you could say that. Though in a way *I* belong to *it* rather than the other way round. But yes, I am the rector of St Bardolph's.' He was leading them back out of the wooded area and into the sunlight. 'I had a parish on the edge of Bristol before this. Very different,' he confessed. The rector was a tall, thin man with a beaky nose, and he looked as though he was close to retirement. 'Bit of a change of pace, I have to say.'

'Have there been many shipwrecks?' Sarah asked.

'I believe so. The rocks just offshore are quite treacherous. Hence the lighthouse. Not necessary now, of course, with modern technology and so on.'

'Many other monuments?' Arthur wondered.

'Strangely not. The *Kairos* was a special case. Partly because some of the crew survived the shipwreck, I gather. At least for a few hours. The records are a little vague. Some accounts say there were nine crew, others eight. The monument, as you can see, names seven sailors. I suppose the villagers who rescued them felt more ... involved.' They had stopped outside the church door and the rector took a large key from his pocket. 'I keep it locked out of habit as much as anything. Old habits, and all that.' He jiggled the key in the lock until he was satisfied, then gave it a sharp twist. 'Then, of course, there was the treasure.'

Arthur and Sarah exchanged glances, then followed him inside.

'Er,' Arthur said, 'treasure?'

'On the *Kairos*. Salvaged by the villagers.' The rector was turning on the lights as he spoke. The inside of the church – wooden pews and plain whitewashed walls with a flagstone floor – echoed. 'It enabled the men to buy their own boats and repair the harbour. Before that they crewed for the fishermen in Tollport. That's the story, anyway.' He smiled at them, pleased at their interest. 'Maybe it's true. Or maybe it's all apocryphal.'

'You think it might all be made up?' Arthur asked him.

'Not all of it. Certainly there was enough money to build the tower, that I do know from the parish records.'

'The church tower?'

'Completed in 1848.'

'Why was it built away from the church?' Sarah asked. 'Because it was new?'

'It's in the same style,' Arthur pointed out.

'The plans show it attached to the chancel,' the rector said. 'There is even the outline of a door over there.' He nodded at a distant corner of the church.

'So what happened?'

'I really couldn't tell you. Legend has it that the villagers did actually build the tower adjoining the church. But during the night after it was completed the Devil himself came and moved it.'

He looked at them closely, as if to gauge their reactions. Sarah laughed.

'Quite. And according to the legend, they took the tower down stone by stone and rebuilt it next to the church again. But the same thing happened. Three times in all.' The old rector chuckled himself at this. 'Things often happen in threes in legends, don't they? But as for the real reason, I'm afraid that is lost in the mists of antiquity. Along with the names of the survivors. If indeed there were any.' He shook their hands again as he excused himself. 'Feel free to look around, please. But I need to get things ready for the morning service tomorrow.'

Arthur and Sarah spent a few minutes walking round the church, out of politeness rather than interest.

'Thank you,' Arthur called out as they left and the rector waved his hand in the air to show he had heard.

Outside it was starting to rain and the wind was getting stronger. It caught the church door as Arthur went to close it, pulling it from his grip and slamming it shut.

As they left the churchyard, hurrying because of the rain, Arthur looked back at the wooded area. He thought he could just see the angels kneeling at the otherwise unmarked graves of the shipwrecked sailors, and he imagined the rain dripped from the remaining angel's head. Tears washing away her face . . .

Chapter 4

The moment the door slammed, Meg knew she was in trouble. She was already halfway out of the front room and had her coat on. She had said goodbye to her mother and was supposed to be meeting Flinch at the den in a few minutes.

Her only hope was that her father would go straight out through the kitchen to the toilet in the yard. But it was early for him to be home from the pub – he must have come direct from work. She stepped back from the door, pushing it quietly closed. She could hear heavy footsteps in the hallway outside.

Her mother was looking up anxiously from the sofa. She rose slowly to her feet, smoothing down her dress with nervous hands.

'You go and see your friends, Meg. I'll be all right.' She spoke quietly. Meg's mother always spoke quietly. She only ever raised her voice behind a closed door and even then it was nothing beside her father's.

The door opened suddenly, hitting the arm of the couch and bouncing back so that Meg's father had to stop it with the flat of his hand. He was a big man and almost filled the doorway as he stood in it, swaying slightly. He saw Meg as soon as he stepped – staggered – into the room.

'Where have you been?' he demanded, staring at her with glassy eyes.

'Nowhere,' she replied in a voice so quiet it was almost a whisper.

'Where have *you* been?' Meg's mother countered. 'Not at work.'

'Left early. Afternoon off. Got a big order.'

'Been celebrating?'

His eyes narrowed and he sank down on the sofa where his wife had been sitting. 'Reckon I have. We all have. Dinner ready?'

'Not yet.'

'I'll get it,' Meg offered quickly. She could smell the beer on his breath and the tobacco on his clothes. She wanted to get out of the room, even if it meant letting Flinch down. Flinch would understand if Meg had to stay in and help her mum. Again.

'No, Meg,' her mother told her. 'You get along. I'll do it.' She met Meg's gaze and Meg could see the dead emptiness inside. 'Just go,' her mother said when Meg hesitated.

'Are you sure you don't need help?' Meg glanced at her father, slumped on the sofa. Her mother followed her gaze, assessing the man's condition.

'I'm sure. I'll be in the kitchen, getting dinner.'

Meg nodded. With another glance at her father, she leaned forward and kissed her mother lightly on the cheek.

'Don't be too long.' There was the ghost of a tremor in her voice.

Meg nodded, blinked and turned to go.

'Where's she off to?' Meg's father demanded.

'To see her friends.'

'Friends? What sort of friends? At this time? Where?'

Meg did not trust herself to answer. She was already in the hall and the door clicked shut behind her. Her mother must have pushed it closed. Meg could hear her voice answering calmly, though she could not make out the words.

Her father's reply was a bellow of rage. A moment later the door opened again and Meg's mother ran out. Her hand was to her mouth, and her eyes were wide in anger and fear. She slammed the door shut behind her.

She and Meg stood staring at each other for several seconds.

'Just go,' Meg's mother said again. 'He'll be asleep soon.'

'I won't be long. Really I won't. You'll be all right?'

'Of course I will.' Her mother turned towards the kitchen. 'I'll be all right.'

Meg went slowly down to the front door. As she opened it, she heard her mother's quiet voice as she said sadly to herself, 'I'm always all right.'

Flinch could tell that Meg was worried about something and she could guess what it was.

'Let's be as quick as we can,' Meg said. 'I want to get back home.'

They were halfway along Berrington Street. The house they wanted would be a little further down, on the other side of the road.

'You remember what Art said we should tell them?'

Flinch nodded. 'I remember.'

'Good. Let me do the talking.'

Flinch wondered why she had to remember what to say if it was Meg who was going to say it. But she knew better than to ask with Meg in her current mood.

The houses in this part of London were large and expensive. Some of them even had small, neat front gardens. But the one they were looking for did not, the area behind the iron railings at the front being paved. The gate opened easily and silently for Flinch, and she stepped aside to let Meg go first.

'Right,' Meg said, reaching for the bell. 'You nervous?'

Flinch nodded quickly. She had no idea who would answer, or what Meg would say. She was glad Meg was doing the talking.

Meg seemed as relieved as Flinch when the door was opened by a young woman. She looked about twenty-five years old. Her hair was tied back and she was wearing a rather old-fashioned dark jacket and skirt, but she seemed pleasant enough.

She smiled slightly as she asked, 'What can I do for you, young ladies?'

Flinch giggled, and Meg nudged her.

'Er,' Meg said. "Well . . .'

'We're from the clock shop,' Flinch said. 'Sorry,' she added quickly, looking at Meg. She had not meant to say anything. It had just slipped out.

'Clock shop?' A shadow passed over the woman's face. 'You mean . . . Edax Rerum?'

'That's right.' Meg seemed to have recovered. 'They asked us to check up on old customers. Well,' she said quickly, 'not that you're old.'

'Checking up on customers?' She seemed worried at the suggestion.

'Customer satisfaction,' Meg suggested.

'I see.'

'Yes,' Meg went on quickly, 'we were given this address for a Miss Wimbourne. But perhaps she's moved. I mean, it was a long time ago.'

The woman was nodding slowly. 'And you just want to know if she is still happy with the clock?'

'That's right,' Flinch told her. 'That's all.'

'Yes,' the woman said, with evident relief. 'Yes, the clock's still fine. Thank you.'

'It's still working, then?' Meg asked.

The woman frowned. 'Of course. Obviously.' Then she smiled again. 'I'm sorry, I wasn't expecting to be asked about it. Not after so long. I was a child, you see, when my father bought the clock for me.'

'For you?' Meg said in surprise. 'You mean you're Miss Wimbourne?'

The woman nodded. 'He used all his savings. But he was so proud. So proud of his little girl . . .' She seemed to be staring into the distance as she spoke. Then she looked directly at Flinch and smiled again. Flinch smiled back. 'I was thinking how young you are to be quizzing customers about their clocks. But I suppose we're all a little older than we look, aren't we?'

'S'pose so,' Flinch said, though she did not really understand what the woman meant.

'Is that all? Or do you need to see the clock?'

Meg hesitated, seemed to consider. 'No,' she said after a moment. 'No, that's all, thank you, Miss Wimbourne.'

Without looking at Flinch, Meg turned and started back down the road.

'She seemed like a nice lady,' Flinch said as she caught up.

'Mmm.'

'Don't you think so? She was very helpful.'

'Mmm,' Meg said again. 'I couldn't tell she was lying.' Meg was frowning, her face lined with concentration. 'But she must have been.'

'Must she?'

'She can't have been Miss Wimbourne. She can't have been given the clock as a child.'

'Why not?'

Meg stopped and turned towards Flinch. 'Because that clock was sold in 1887,' she said. 'Even if she was given it the day she was born, she would have to be . . .' Meg looked away as she worked it out. 'She would have to be fifty years old.'

'Get out,' the old man shouted. 'Get out before I set the dog on you!' The threat was curtailed by a fit of coughing. There was no sign of a dog.

'We're going,' Art assured him.

Jonny was already gone. Art joined him on the pavement as the old man slammed the door shut. A moment later his wrinkled face appeared at the window of the front room, staring at the boys.

'What's up with him?' Jonny wondered.

Art shrugged. 'Search me.'

The window slid noisily open and the old man's head poked out at them, like a wrinkled turtle coming out of its shell. 'Had that clock for my tenth birthday,' he shouted. Art could see that his cheeks were wet with tears. 'Nothing but trouble, that clock. Cursed, my sister says. If I could get rid of it, I would.' The head withdrew. 'Get away from here. Just go away,' the old man's cracked voice called out. Then the window was slammed shut.

'He's going ga-ga,' Jonny told Art as they set off for the den. 'Tenth birthday.'

Jonny had probably done the sums more quickly than Art. According to the sales ledger, the clock had been sold to George Rollason for his son Henry in 1889. If the man was ten in 1889, he would be nearly sixty now. Old, but not that old. The man they had just met – the man who claimed to be Henry Rollason, son of George – was at least ninety.

They spent Sunday in St Ives. Arthur and Sarah went off on their own, leaving Dad to make some notes for his report, but the shops Sarah wanted to look at were not the ones Arthur was interested in. So he left her to get on with it and found a book shop.

Monday was cold and foggy. Dad didn't fancy driving and suggested they try the village pub. Arthur was keen to take a look at the lighthouse museum. Sarah seemed happy to do both.

It was eerie walking in the fog. The main street through the village was cobbled and was slick with the damp. The pub was halfway round the harbour, with views out over the bay – when you could see more than about ten metres in front of you. But it wasn't open yet. Arthur's dad found a notice with opening times.

'Another hour.'

'The lighthouse opens at ten,' Arthur told them. 'It says so on the leaflet.'

'Even in February?'

'That's what it said.'

The pub sign was a painting of a sailing ship wrecked on the beach. Shadowy figures were walking from it, carrying its cargo inland — barrels and crates on their shoulders. Water dripped off the sign where the fog had condensed, so it seemed like the sea in the painting was leaking into the real world.

'Looks like one of Sladden's,' Sarah remarked. 'A painter we met on the beach,' she told Arthur's dad.

'It's a very old sign,' he replied. 'See how the paint has cracked and faded.'

The lighthouse loomed above them out of the fog. The road that led up to it was deserted. From its shadowy silhouette, Arthur thought they might be approaching the tower of a medieval castle rather than a Victorian lighthouse.

'It doesn't look very open,' Dad said.

There was no light, no sign of life. Not even a car in the little car park. The door was shut.

'We might as well try now we're here.'

The door opened easily, to reveal a room that took up the whole of the base of the tower. A steep stone staircase ran up the far wall, twisting round the outer wall. There was a table with leaflets and guidebooks just inside the door. A figure in the uniform, Arthur guessed, of a nineteenth-century lighthouse keeper stood stiff and still against one wall. A model ship in a glass display case looked in need of paint and attention. A sign pointed up the stairs: 'Exhibition Areas'.

There was another figure sitting immobile on a chair at the foot of the stairs. He was dressed in a shabby suit and was holding a book. Arthur thought at first this was another mannequin, but the man looked up as they entered. He snapped the book shut and stood up.

He was a middle-aged man with greasy dark hair that was combed across his head in an effort to disguise how thin it was getting on the top. His face was round and looked like it was used to smiling. He was smiling now.

'Visitors, how splendid.' The man rubbed his hands together and blinked several times. 'We don't get many visitors this time of year. Or in this weather. You're staying locally?'

Arthur left his dad to explain and sort out paying. He went to examine the lighthouse keeper, looking for a notice that might say who he was and what period he was from. But there was nothing.

'Not impressed so far,' Sarah murmured close to his ear.

'No,' he agreed. 'Still, at least it's open.'

'Would you like me to come round with you and explain everything?' the man asked eagerly. 'Or you could take a guidebook. It's very full, though I say so myself. I wrote it, you see. At least, the latest edition. Malcolm Brown,' he announced proudly, struggling to impress.

'I think we'll be all right, thank you,' Arthur's dad told him, much to Arthur's relief. 'But we'll give you a call if we have any questions.'

'Of course, of course.' Malcolm Brown rubbed his hands together in satisfaction. 'Anything at all. There are small exhibitions in the rooms, showing how the lighthouse would have been at various times in its history. Er, not that there's much of that, I'm afraid. But the lamp room is given over to a smuggling exhibition which I dare say you'll find even more interesting.'

'No lamp?' Sarah asked.

Malcolm Brown looked embarrassed. 'Alas, no. That was removed when the lighthouse was decommissioned in 1973.' His tone brightened as he told her, 'We did look into getting a replica made,

63

from the original specification.' His face fell again. 'But sadly the cost was prohibitive. We do have a fund, but there's a long way to go yet.' He made a point of glancing over at a metal collecting box attached to the wall close to the main door.

At intervals up the stairs there were rooms. They were all gloomy and cramped, with curving walls and low ceilings. Most of them were sparsely furnished, and all had at least one unconvincing mannequin posed in an attempt to show how the room might have looked when occupied by real people. Arthur and Sarah spared most of them little more than a glance, but Arthur's dad insisted on reading the information board on the wall just inside each room. So they left him to it and kept going.

They looked in at a room with bunk beds and a small wardrobe. They glanced at a small sitting room with a circular table and upright chairs where two mannequins were eating plastic lunch. Arthur spent slightly longer in the telegraph room, where a sprawling figure was supposed to be sending a message, though its attention was obviously elsewhere and its hand had come detached from the telegraph.

Eventually they found themselves arriving at the top of the staircase and in the lamp room. It was smaller than the room at the base of the tower, but with a high ceiling. It was much lighter, being glassed in all round. Arthur could see a narrow balcony running round outside, but not much more because the fog was so thick it seemed to be pressing in on the glass.

The smuggling exhibition was rather more comprehensive than he had expected from the rooms they had seen up till now. There were display stands with printed boards on them, model ships and a relief map of the local area with arrows showing where ships had been wrecked and where smugglers would bring in their contraband unobserved. Old photographs showed various coves and caves and supposed hiding places. There were sketches and engravings of the more famous smugglers, and a reprinted article from a local paper explaining how 'wrecking' was a myth and the closest anyone ever came to deliberately luring a ship on to the rocks was looting ships that had already managed to run aground without any extra help.

There was another, equally dilapidated, model

boat in a similar display case to the one downstairs. It was, in the process of being unconvincingly smashed to pieces on the rocks. Some of the rocks that jutted up from the papier-mâché sea had become detached and could be seen to be made of polystyrene, which did nothing to help the illusion.

'So that's it,' Sarah said, joining Arthur by the display case. She pointed to the name at the bottom of the model: 'Kairos, 1843'. 'And have you seen the paintings over there?' she asked. 'They're all by Martin Sladden.'

There were about a dozen paintings, arranged in a little exhibition area of their own. A small plaque mentioned that Martin Sladden was a celebrated local artist who specialised in seascapes and had a studio in Porthellis.

All the paintings showed ships at sea – some in calm waters, others tossed by stormy waves. Several were being hurled against the rocks or dashed on the shore. It was just an impression, nothing specific in the painting apart from the way the light fell and the sails were curled, but in several of the pictures Arthur was sure the main mast of the ship was topped with a flag – the skull and crossbones.

One showed a ship crashing against a rocky shoreline, painted as if seen by a doomed sailor on the ship. It was a powerful painting, and Arthur could well imagine the fear and desperation of the crew as they clung to the disintegrating rigging or fell headlong into the turbulent waters. The whole picture was angled as if the painter was at that moment being flung across the deck. In the distance the dark cliffs were just visible, a fire burning on the top of one and lighting the sky above it a deep orange. Perhaps it had been lit in a futile effort to warn the ship away from the treacherous rocks.

As he turned to move on, Arthur noticed a picture at the side of the display that was not a seascape. It seemed to have been deliberately pushed to one side, as if whoever had set up the display had not been sure what to do with it. The painting showed the interior of a room. It was an old room with low beams. The centrepiece was a fireplace, with chairs either side of it and a dog stretched out on the hearth. The fire was burning brightly and the flames looked to Arthur like storm-whipped waves of orange and yellow.

But what held Arthur's attention was a single detail, one object in the very centre of the painting, standing on the mantel above the fire. It was a clock. A simple, wooden clock. Except that instead of numerals, the dial was marked with the signs of the zodiac. Instead of hands, a sun and a moon orbited the dial.

Chapter 5

'It could just be coincidence,' Art had suggested.

'Two nutcases who happen to have clocks from that shop, you mean?' Jonny said.

'She was a nice lady,' Flinch offered.

'Just bad at mathematics, perhaps.'

'Thank you, Jonny.' Art turned to Meg. 'What do you think?'

She seemed surprised to be asked. 'Me? I . . .' She considered, biting at her lower lip. 'I don't know. It's odd, but there's probably nothing in it.'

Art nodded. 'That's what I think.'

'So we just drop it?' Jonny was disappointed.

'No, I think we need to investigate a bit further. To be sure.' Art grinned. 'Like you said, we may just have found a couple of nutcases.' He opened his casebook and ran a finger down the list he had copied from the ledger in the shop. 'How about tomorrow afternoon, Jonny and I try this Dr John Smith in Streatham. You up to another visit, Meg?'

She nodded. Beside her, Flinch was also nodding enthusiastically.

'Good. There's a Roderick Bartlett in Vicarage Square. Why don't you give that a go?'

* * *

Vicarage Square was a small courtyard set back from the main road. There was only one house on the square. Meg said maybe it used to be the vicarage, but Flinch was not sure about that. It seemed a long way from any church.

'Are you going to do all the talking again?' Flinch asked when they reached the large front door.

Meg pulled the bell. The sound was only faintly audible as the bell rang somewhere deep within the house. They waited for what seemed an age before Flinch heard the heavy tread of someone approaching. Moments later the door was opened.

Flinch almost gasped, but managed to control herself. The man who opened the door was small, not much taller than Flinch herself. He seemed even shorter because he was stooped, his arms hanging forwards so they reached below his bent knees. Behind him, the twin tails of his suit jacket hung down just as low, so that he looked like a dark, six-legged spider. His face was lined with age and his grey hair had receded to the point where it was almost non-existent. A few surviving strands were oiled across the top of his head – and because he was so bent, it was the top that was the most visible part of his head. He seemed to make an effort to look up, and small, dark eyes glistened within the wrinkled face.

'Can I help you?' His voice was surprisingly strong and deep. He turned slowly, his feet not moving but his arms and coat-tails swinging with his body.

Meg cleared her throat, clearly as surprised at the butler's appearance as Flinch was. 'We were hoping to speak to Mr Bartlett.'

The butler raised his head slightly more, craning to see Meg's face. Flinch saw his little eyes widen in sudden astonishment. His mouth opened, the dry skin at the corners unpeeling as the gap between his lips widened.

He stood frozen, staring at Meg, who shuffled uncomfortably under his gaze.

At that moment a voice called from inside the house. If the butler's voice had been strong and deep, this voice was even more assured and in every way darker and richer.

'Who is it, Crow?'

Immediately the butler snapped to a sort of

attention. His body straightened up slightly and Flinch almost expected him to salute.

'Some people to see you, sir.'

'Do I want to see them?' the voice wondered.

At the end of the hallway, Flinch could see the dark figure of a tall, lean man. He was walking slowly towards them. The butler stepped aside as he approached.

The contrast between the little hunched butler and his tall master made Flinch want to laugh. But she could see that the man was as surprised as his servant had been at the sight of the two girls.

'I see,' he said slowly. For several seconds he stared at Meg. This time she stared back defiantly, until he went on, 'I'm so sorry. I don't often get such pleasant visitors.' The man smiled. 'I am Roderick Bartlett, is it me that you wish to see?' He gestured for the butler to leave them, and the little man lurched away down the hall, into the shadows.

While Meg went through her routine about being from the clock shop, Flinch watched Roderick Bartlett. He was a young man and he stood like a soldier on parade. He was tall and his face was long. His dark hair was carefully parted in the middle and he had a neatly trimmed beard. His fingers, Flinch noticed, were also long – even his fingernails looked long.

'Why don't you step inside and see the clock for yourself?' Bartlett said as Meg finished. 'It's just here, in the hall.'

He stood aside and motioned for Meg to come in. Flinch made to follow, but Bartlett was already closing the door. He seemed to notice Flinch at the last moment, and just for a second, just before he seemed to relent and open the door again for her, Flinch thought his face twisted into a mask of anger. But then he smiled and stepped aside once more for Flinch.

'I'm sorry, I didn't catch your names.'

'I'm Flinch and that's Meg.'

'Meg.' Bartlett nodded. 'Short for Megan, perhaps?'

'Margaret,' Meg corrected him. 'Margaret Wallace. Is this the clock?'

It was an old grandfather clock, standing in an alcove in the hallway. Because it was set back from the hall, the clock was in shadow and it would have been easy to miss seeing it at all. The

73

case was dark wood, the clock face a dull bronze colour. The hands were set at exactly seven o'clock and Flinch could not hear it ticking.

'It's stopped,' she said. 'Does it need winding up?'

Bartlett's attention still seemed to be on Meg, and even when he answered, he did not look at Flinch. 'It doesn't go. I keep it for . . .' He paused, as if unsure quite why he did keep the clock. 'For sentimental reasons,' he decided. He was smiling thinly. 'I have no complaints. It has been in the family for some years now, as I expect you know. My grandfather bought it, in 1855 I believe.'

Meg nodded. 'Yes. Thank you. That's very helpful.'

'Look,' Bartlett said as Meg turned back towards the door, 'I'm about to have some tea. Will you join me?' He glanced at Flinch, then straight back at Meg. 'Both of you?'

There was something about the way he said it, the way he included her almost as an afterthought, that made Flinch wary. She could see Meg was hesitating, obviously tempted by the offer. She seemed to like the man and might accept. But Flinch had already decided she did not like Roderick Bartlett. 'No thanks,' she said before Meg could reply. 'We have to go. Sorry. Our friends are expecting us.'

Bartlett ignored her. 'You don't have to stay long,' he told Meg. 'But if it is inconvenient, perhaps tomorrow? You could bring your friends,' he added as Meg still did not answer.

Flinch did not wait. She walked briskly back to the front door and yanked it open. As she did, the clock began to strike. She counted. Seven – it struck seven.

'I thought you said it didn't work,' she called back to Bartlett.

The man was still looking at Meg. 'The hands don't move,' he said. 'But sometimes it strikes.'

'Come on Meg.' Flinch stepped outside.

Meg joined her a few moments later.

'That man was creepy,' Flinch said.

'Do you think so?' Meg said nothing more the whole way back to the den.

Jonny and Art were already waiting for them. Their Dr Smith had apparently moved years ago and left no forwarding address. It was only after

75

they had told the girls in detail about how they had tried, and failed, to track him down that Meg told them about the visit to Roderick Bartlett.

'And so,' she finished, as Flinch listened in disbelief, 'I said we'd all go round for tea tomorrow.'

The fog had thinned by the time they left the lighthouse and Arthur was astonished to realise that it was already gone one o'clock.

They made their way back down to the village, buildings looming out of the grey air as dark ghosts before becoming substantial and recognisable. There was one main street, which followed the harbour round. Several other roads came off it, but none of them were very wide or long or went anywhere. Arthur glanced along several, seeing the vague outlines of houses and the occasional shop.

On one corner was Sladden's studio. It took Arthur a moment to realise that it was not just another house. But there were paintings hung in the window and a sign above the door.

'Shall we have a look?' he suggested.

'Best get to the pub,' Dad said. 'They might finish lunch at two.'

'Just a quick look,' Arthur promised. 'I'll catch you up.' He turned to Sarah, but she made a face and shook her head. She was probably cold, looking forward to sitting in the warmth of the pub.

He knew as soon as he walked in. The beams were still there, though the fireplace had gone, replaced with a cupboard. But Arthur could tell it was the same room he had seen in the painting at the lighthouse. There was still a shelf where the mantelpiece had been, but now it had pots of paintbrushes on it. A desk stood to one side, with papers piled up beside a telephone.

A bell jangled as he closed the door behind him and a moment later Martin Sladden came through from a back room, rubbing his hands on a cloth.

'Hello again, young man.'

'I saw your paintings up at the lighthouse,' Arthur told him.

'What did you think?'

'Good. Very impressive.' Arthur looked round. 'One of them is of this room, isn't it?'

Sladden frowned. 'I didn't know Brown had put that one out.'

'You usually do ships, though, don't you?'

'Usually.'

'But I recognised the room. From the beams. What happened to the clock?' he asked casually – not because he wanted to know, just to make conversation.

'There is no clock,' Sladden snapped angrily. 'There never was any clock. It's just a painting. A fiction. All right?'

For a moment they both stood in embarrassed silence.

'All right.' Arthur was surprised at the man's outburst. 'I'm sorry. Look, I'd better be going. I'm supposed to be having lunch at the pub with my dad.'

Sladden nodded, having apparently recovered his good humour. 'The pasties are good,' he said. 'But don't have the coffee. It tastes like tar.'

He was right about the coffee. Arthur didn't have any, but his dad did. He drank half and left the rest.

'It tastes of tar,' Arthur said.

'You're not wrong. How did you know?'

'Everyone round here knows that.'

'Must be traditional,' Sarah said. 'Like the menu.'

The food was good, though. Apart from the Cornish pasty, each of the dishes had been given what Arthur's dad had called a 'traditional' name. Fish and chips became 'Smuggler's Catch' and bangers and mash was for some reason 'Pirate's Booty'.

They sat and chatted for a while after lunch. From the window Arthur could tell it was still foggy and cold. None of them seemed in any hurry to get back, and the pub was open all day. The landlord and his wife, or possibly she was his sister, were attentive and friendly. Arthur, Sarah and Dad had the Family Room to themselves, but the public bar was full of locals laughing and drinking and eating.

Arthur's dad was keen to find out from Sarah all about what her mother had been up to for the past few years – where her job was going, what she was doing in America, everything. Arthur found it all a bit boring. But there was a shelf of books in the Family Room that included a couple of local guides and so he flicked through these and made the odd comment.

One of the books included a chapter on Porthellis Church and recounted the legend of the Devil moving the tower. Arthur read bits of it out, and he and Sarah told Dad about their meeting with the rector and finding the monument to the shipwrecked sailors of the *Kairos*.

It was getting dark by the time Dad suggested they should be making for home. 'I'd better get started on writing up my report. Oh,' he said, suddenly remembering as he took his coat from the back of the chair, 'but you wanted to have a proper look in that gallery, didn't you?'

'If it's still open.' He didn't really want to any more, but he wasn't ready to go back to the cottage yet. 'It's all right, Dad. You don't need to come.'

'OK,' Dad agreed. 'If you're sure. Sarah?'

'I'll go with Arthur,' Sarah said.

The lights were on in the studio, blurring out through the foggy darkness that surrounded it. They stood at the window, looking at the paintings on display.

'Look at the prices,' Sarah said. 'I want to get mum a present. But it won't be a painting.'

'I thought that was the date,' Arthur said with a laugh.

'Or his phone number.'

Between the paintings, they could see into the room beyond. They saw Sladden come in from the back room and Arthur waved. But the man did not see them. He seemed distracted, pacing backwards and forwards in front of his desk.

'Shall we go in?' Sarah asked. She took a step towards the door.

But Arthur caught her hand and held her back. 'No, wait.'

'Why?'

'I'm not sure. It's just . . .' He shrugged. 'I don't know.'

In the room, Sladden had stopped pacing. He glanced furtively over at the window, but because it was dark outside he did not seem to be able to see Sarah and Arthur. He stooped down in front of the cupboard where the fireplace had been in the painting.

'What's he up to?' Sarah wondered.

He had the cupboard open now, was reaching inside, rummaging round for something. But whatever it was, there were other things in the way. Arthur and Sarah watched as Sladden pulled out a roll of canvas and put it to one side. Next a metal box, then a pile of papers. He paused, as if wondering whether it was worth continuing, then carefully, almost delicately, he took something else from the cupboard. It looked heavy. He carried it to the desk and perched it on top of the pile of papers beside the phone.

It was a clock.

He had placed it so it was facing the window – a clock in a square wooden case, with symbols round the dial instead of numbers, the sun and moon instead of hands. It was the clock from the painting.

Arthur realised, embarrassed, that he was still holding Sarah's hand, and let it go. She glanced at him, as if she had not realised either.

'Is that like your clock?' she asked. 'The clock you told me about?' For some reason she was whispering.

'No,' he whispered back. 'But, I don't know, somehow it reminds me of it.'

Sladden had taken something else from the cupboard now. Arthur almost laughed when he saw what it was – a bottle of whisky. The painter straightened up, pulling out the cork and swigging from the bottle.

'Perhaps it's best not to disturb him right now,' Arthur said.

'I think you're right.'

Whether Sladden caught sight of them at the window as they turned, or some trick of the light threw a reflection into the room, or he caught the distant sound of approaching thunder, Arthur never knew. But as they turned to go, Sladden took a surprised step backwards, the bottle still half-tipped in front of him. His leg hit the chair by the desk and he put his free hand out to steady himself.

The hand caught the desk, knocked it. The stack of papers slid sideways, taking the clock with it. Slowly, but inexorably, the clock also slid sideways. Sladden saw it moving, overreacted, tried to grab it, but succeeded only in pushing it away.

Even outside the shop, even above the sound of the gathering storm, Arthur and Sarah heard his cry of anger and surprise.

The clock toppled from the desk, twisted in the air and landed face down on the floor. Arthur imagined he could hear the glass over the clock face cracking. But it was the crack of thunder. The evening was illuminated with lightning, jagged stabs of light reaching through the fog and sending it swirling away in tatters.

'Come on.' Arthur grabbed Sarah's hand again, all embarrassment gone, and together they ran along the street, back towards the cottage.

There was no trace of the fog now. Just a dark sky split by silver lightning, the growing rumble of thunder and the sudden driving rain.

Chapter 6

Tea was an extraordinary affair. Art was not sure quite what to make of Roderick Bartlett. He seemed pleasant enough, greeting the Cannoniers at the door and leading them through a large hallway to the drawing room. They passed the grandfather clock standing in an alcove outside the drawing room, as Meg had described. Sure enough, it seemed to have stopped, the hand motionless at a little before five past seven. '*Tempus non fugit*', it said on the dial.

In the drawing room, tea was already set out, and the butler was waiting patiently to pour. He was stooped and old, and it seemed to Art that the weight of the silver teapot the man held was dragging him down. If he stood there much longer, he might collapse into the floor.

If anything, the man was too attentive – arranging and rearranging the tea things as soon as any of them put anything down, topping up their cups whether they wanted more tea or not.

Art and Jonny spent much of the time exchanging glances. Flinch was heavily involved in fruit cake, accepting slice after slice without comment. From the way she looked sideways at Bartlett, Art could tell she was not impressed by him.

Meg, on the other hand, spoke and smiled and laughed with Bartlett in a way which Art had never seen before. She caught his eye at one point and a guilty frown flickered across her face, as if he had seen her doing something she should not. But Bartlett was the perfect host to Meg, sat beside her on the chaise longue and continually asking if she was comfortable, whether she wanted more tea or cake, how she found school, what she thought of the weather at this time of year . . .

Jonny made a point of watching Meg and Bartlett closely and attentively, his head moving to follow their conversation like a tennis match. But after a while he seemed to realise what Art had known almost at once – that Roderick Bartlett was not the slightest bit interested in any of them apart from Meg. Bartlett made no comment when Jonny got up and started to walk round the room, examining the furnishings, the pictures, the ornaments.

Crow glared at Art as he stood up and went to

join Jonny on the far side of the room. Art smiled back at the man, and saw his eyes narrow in annoyance.

'Meg's having fun,' Jonny said quietly to Art.

'So's Flinch. Have you seen how much cake she's eaten?'

'Six slices,' Jonny said without looking round. 'Probably seven by now.' He did glance back now, a quick look at Meg and Bartlett. 'Nice man,' he said levelly.

Art shrugged. 'Seems to be. And it was Meg he invited to tea, we're just her friends.'

Jonny did not answer. He picked up a small wooden box from a side table, turning it over in his hands before putting it down again.

'Careful,' Art murmured. 'We don't want to break anything.'

Beside the box was a small photograph frame. It was the sort that held two photographs and stood up like a birthday card so that the portraits seemed to be angled to face each other. Jonny picked it up, opened it to glance at the pictures – a sepia-toned man and a woman – then put it back again.

'Hang on,' Jonny said suddenly, and snatched

the picture frame back from the table. He opened it and held it for Art to see. 'Remind you of anyone?'

Art looked at the man. It was an old photograph, faded and slightly out of focus. Even behind the glass it looked brittle. The man stared back at Art, stiffly posed. He had a long face with a thin nose and dark hair parted in the middle.

'Looks like Bartlett,' Art admitted. 'His father maybe. Or grandfather – it's a very old picture.'

Jonny angled the frame, tapping the other photograph with his finger. 'Not him, I mean *her*.'

The other portrait was of a young woman. She looked as stiff and brittle as the man, staring back at Art through eyes paled with age. She looked as if she was in her early twenties, with a mass of curly hair that framed a slightly sullen face. Art had to admit, it did remind him of someone. The hair in particular. Who did he know with hair like that – only hair that was not brown.

Across the room, Meg laughed at something Bartlett had said. It was strange to hear her genuinely happy. Art looked round, startled at the sound. He saw Bartlett gesturing for Crow to pour more tea, saw Meg holding her cup out, saw she was smiling. He saw the mass of red curls that cascaded over her shoulders, framing her face. And he knew who the photograph reminded him of . . .

At that moment, Bartlett turned. He glared across the room at Art and Jonny. Art hoped Jonny had put the photographs down. His eyes met Bartlett's and he almost felt the man's anger. But Bartlett's face cleared, and he smiled thinly and, Art suspected, reluctantly. The man ran a hand through his hair, pushing it back over his head. It flopped back as soon as he moved his hand away. But the second for which Bartlett's forehead had been visible had been enough for Art and Jonny both to see the red birthmark on the left side – a dark discoloration in the shape of an uneven star.

The butler, Crow, was clearing away the tea. Flinch only realised what he was doing when she reached for another piece of cake – just one more – and found that the plate had gone. She looked round quickly and saw the dark spider-like shape of the man disappearing through the door.

Flinch did not like the house, or the room, or the people. But the cake had been good and now that it was gone she wanted another piece more than ever. Bartlett's attention seemed to be completely focused on Meg, and Flinch did not want to have to ask him to have the cake brought back anyway. Jonny and Art were on the other side of the room, talking quietly and looking at ornaments and pictures. Nobody seemed to be paying her any attention and Crow had gone.

So she got up and followed him out. She thought the man was creepy, but it was his job to serve the cake. So she would tell him she had not finished. The hallway was empty, so she headed towards the back of the house, where she guessed the kitchens would be. In a house as big as this there would be servants' quarters and probably a cook. She could hear Crow's shoes on the wooden floor ahead of her as she followed him.

But there was no kitchen. At least, not the way that Flinch had gone. She must have missed the door, as she found herself in a long, narrow corridor with thick, dark carpet on the floor. Crow's footsteps would have made no sound if he had come this way.

As Flinch turned to retrace her steps, deciding that perhaps she would have to give up the idea of more cake, she found she was facing a door. On a whim, without really thinking, she opened it and looked into the room beyond.

It was dark. The curtains were drawn, and a little light seeped round the edges and through the material where it seemed to have worn away. As her eyes adjusted, Flinch could see that it was a small sitting room. But it obviously had not been used for some time – years, probably. The whole room was coated in a layer of dust.

There was a round table in the centre of the room, with a chair beside it. On the chair, as if it had been left only minutes before, was a sampler. A needle was sticking up from it. Flinch walked slowly and cautiously over to the table. She could see now that someone had been embroidering the sampler with a pattern of flowers. Once they had been brightly coloured, but now they were all a uniform grey. The needle was dull and rusty. A book was lying on the table, a faded ribbon for a bookmark.

The room was stuffy – musty and stale. Flinch went over to the window, pulling the curtain aside to let in some light. A layer of dust scattered over her hand and she let go again. But the dust had got in her nose, making her want to sneeze. She didn't like it and gently pulled the curtain again.

It was a sash window that opened by pushing upwards. But there was a catch at the top. If she stretched, Flinch could just reach it. The catch was stiff through lack of use, but she managed to undo it. Then she tried to open the window. But that was stiff as well – too stiff for Flinch to open. She abandoned the window. There was no reason to stay in the room anyway.

Flinch shivered. If it were not for the dust and the smell of decay, she could believe someone had been here only moments before. But despite the abandoned needlework, the book, an empty carafe and a stained glass at the back of the table, Flinch knew that she must be the first person to enter the room in years.

There was a portrait hanging on the wall. Flinch saw it as she tiptoed back to the door, hoping she was not leaving footprints in the dust. The painting was dark and obviously old. The heavy plaster frame had been gilded, but now it was almost white with dust.

The woman in the picture was smiling,

despite the gloomy surroundings. Flinch paused, staring at the face, the cascading hair . . . It reminded her of someone she knew – or rather, someone she had seen. Someone she had seen only a few times, at the door of a house, saying goodbye to her daughter, or welcoming her home.

It was the very image of Meg's mother.

It was not long before Arthur decided he was as wet as he could possibly get. At that point he stopped running madly and slowed to a jog.

Beside him, still holding his hand, Sarah was laughing. Arthur realised he was laughing too.

'Come to sunny Cornwall in warm February,' Arthur shouted above the thunder and the rain. His attempt at a Cornish accent was not especially successful, but Sarah laughed all the more.

'Oh, I'm drenched,' she said. 'This is ridiculous.'

They paused to catch their breath on the cliffs between the church and the cottage.

Arthur nodded out to sea. 'Look at it.'

'Spectacular,' Sarah agreed.

The sky was black, with smudges of cloud split by lightning. The waves were white-tipped, crashing down into the sea and breaking heavily on the shore far below them.

'Almost worth getting soaked to see that,' Arthur said.

'Almost. But I'm soaked enough. Come on.'

'No, wait – what's that?' He pointed. On the distant horizon, standing even darker against the black sky, there was a tiny shape. It was moving, pitching and tilting in the storm.

'Is it a ship?'

Arthur strained to see. 'It could be. It looks like . . .' His voice tailed off. He hardly dared to say it. But now it was obviously a ship – an old-fashioned sailing ship, the mast bent and the sails in tatters as it was driven towards the shore. Towards the cliffs and the rocks. It seemed to shimmer against the background of the tossing sea, as if it was somehow catching the lightning.

'It looks like one of those paintings,' Sarah said.

Which was exactly what Arthur had thought. The ship was too far away to see it, but he was certain that if they waited for it to drift closer, he would see the tattered black flag at the top of the mast, the white emblem shredded by the storm. The skull and crossbones.

Arthur's dad was pulling on his coat when they staggered through the door and stood dripping in the cottage's small hallway. They were both wet through and laughing again.

'I was just coming to find you,' Dad said. 'I was afraid you might get wet.'

And with that they were all laughing, almost uncontrollably.

'There's a ship out there,' Arthur said when he recovered. 'At least, I think there is. Could be a trick of the light, I suppose.'

'They should be all right,' Dad said. 'They'll be used to storms, and they'll have maps and a radio.' He looked them up and down and shook his head. 'You'd better both go and get dry. I'll put the kettle on.'

There was a knock at his door as Arthur finished getting dressed in dry clothes. It was Sarah. She was drying her long hair with a towel and had also changed into new clothes – jeans and a pullover.

'There *was* a ship,' she said. She sat down on his bed. 'Weird, isn't it?'

'Just a bit. Did you notice how the storm seemed to start when he dropped the clock?'

She nodded. 'That's what I meant. So where's your clock, then?' She tilted her head to one side and tried to coax the water out of her ear with the towel.

Arthur pulled his holdall out of the small wardrobe. He had unpacked his clothes and books and stuff, but left the clock in the bag. He was not really sure why he had bothered to bring it. It was just a clock after all, and it didn't work. But he pulled it out, angling it to show her the name scratched out on the back.

'And that says "Margaret Wallace"?'

'Yes. At least, I'm pretty sure it does. It's difficult to tell though.' He handed it to her. 'Sorry, it's probably just an ordinary clock.'

The ghosts he had seen, the way the clock had seemed to somehow roll back time itself while he was in the haunted house in London, seemed so far away now. As if it was a dream, or had happened to someone else. He could almost believe he had imagined it all.

'That's not ordinary,' Sarah said. 'Have you wound it up? You said it didn't go.'

Arthur sat down beside her and leaned across to look. Sarah had turned the clock over and was looking at the dial. 'Edax Rerum' was written across the face in stylised Italic script. But that was not what Sarah was looking at. There was another crash of thunder from outside.

'No, it isn't ordinary at all,' Arthur admitted.

The hands of the clock were spinning so fast they were almost a blur. Arthur took the clock from Sarah and put it carefully on the low table beside the bed, next to his alarm clock. The hands continued to spin out of control. Faster and faster. And backwards . . .

Chapter 7

He did not really think there was much point in returning to the clock shop. But Art wanted to talk to Jonny, and the journey to consult the old sales ledger again, supposedly looking for more clues, meant the two boys could have some time together. Flinch was happy to stay at the den that Saturday rather than traipse across London to visit the dusty old shop, and none of them had seen Meg. Probably she was at home with her mother, helping with chores.

'It's a big house,' Art said. 'If there's just Bartlett and Crow there, then I'm not surprised some of the rooms have gone to seed.'

'Bit odd, though,' Jonny said. 'Not just what Flinch said about that painting, but the photograph too.'

'Coincidence?' Art shrugged. 'I'm glad none of us mentioned it to Meg, though. Might have spooked her.'

'Something's spooked her all right,' Jonny muttered.

They had reached the narrow street where the clock shop was situated. 'Look, I'm not sure we really need to look at that ledger again,' Art confessed. 'And without Flinch it'll be a struggle to get back in.'

'No, it won't,' Jonny told him. 'There's a light on inside – look.' He pointed along the road to the shop. There was indeed a light on inside and the door seemed to be standing open. 'There's someone in there.'

'Looking for something in particular?' the old clockmaker asked. His voice grated like rusty cogwheels.

It was the man from the photograph, though where he was standing behind the counter meant he blocked Art and Jonny's view of it. His moustache twitched, flicking slightly upwards, in an almost rhythmic motion.

'We just wanted a look round,' Jonny said.

'We were surprised to see the shop open,' Art admitted. 'We thought it had gone out of business.'

'Not quite out of business,' the clock man said. 'Though it is very slow these days.'

'Like some of the clocks,' Jonny said, laughing nervously.

The clock man did not laugh. 'This shop was established in 1838,' he said. 'Though it wasn't until 1843 that business picked up. Now it seems to have tailed off again . . .' His voice tailed off too, fading into silence.

Art made a pretence of being interested in one of the clocks. It was a simple wooden carriage clock standing on a shelf along with dozens of others. It was as dusty and old as everything else. He wondered vaguely if the clock man's bald head was also filmed with dust, and smiled at the thought.

'I have been away,' the clock man announced suddenly. 'For a while. Now I seem to be back.'

'So we see,' Jonny said. 'Well, good luck with business.' He looked at Art and nodded towards the door.

Art was about to agree that they should go, when the clock man spoke again. '1843,' he repeated. 'That was when the old sea captain came knocking, in the middle of the night.' He stared off into space. 'I remember it as if it were yesterday.'

'Yes,' Art said slowly. 'Well, perhaps we should be on our way.'

'The middle of the night. The shop was closed of course, but I heard him all the same. Made enough noise to wake the dead, hammering on the door with his iron hook.'

Jonny was grinning at this. '1843,' he mouthed to Art, and spun his finger close to his ear. 'Ga-ga,' he whispered.

Art grinned back. Jonny was right. Maybe the man was confused about the date, or was retelling a story his grandfather had told him . . . Or maybe he was just plain round the twist.

'He had the ship's clock with him. Wrapped in an oilskin. The glass across the face was cracked. I had never seen a clock like it. Instead of numerals, the dial was marked with the signs of the zodiac. Instead of hands, a sun and a moon orbited the dial. It was old. You could tell it was old. Such craftsmanship – it looked like it was made only yesterday.' The man shook his head as he seemed to remember.

'It needed mending?' Art asked, intrigued despite himself.

'Been dropped, so he said. The glass across the dial was cracked and the mechanism had been jolted. I asked him where it was from, and he told me he had acquired it – that was the word he used, "acquired" – he had acquired it in the East. He didn't say exactly where, and I didn't ask.' The clock man nodded, fixing Art with his round eyes. 'He was a big man. Not one to argue with. I mentioned his hook? In place of his left hand, that was. Vicious-looking thing. Barbed. His heart was as black as his beard, and he had a sort of sword in his belt. A cutlass. I couldn't make out much detail of his face. It was night, as I say. Dark. He kept to the shadows, and his voice – his voice was a dry rasp, as if he had drunk nothing but sea water for twenty years.'

'Did you . . .' Jonny swallowed. 'Did you mend his clock for him?'

'I did. It wasn't too damaged. I could see at once what the problem was, though the mechanism was like no clock I'd ever seen before. One of the wheels was bent, another had slipped out of alignment. But I was there almost all night with that clock. That wonderful clock.' His eyes were unfocused again, looking back into his memory. 'By the time I was done, I knew every aspect of the mechanism, every detail of the movement.'

The clock man gave a short laugh. 'He told me that was my fee. Didn't offer me money, nor treasure. He said that my looking at the mechanism, my understanding how that clock functioned and being able to duplicate its working, was worth more to me than all the treasure he'd ever "acquired".'

'And was it?' Jonny asked, his eyes wide now he was caught up in the story.

The clock man did not seem to hear. 'Then the first flickerings of dawn began to appear in the sky, and he took his clock and was gone. I suppose he walked out through that door, but I didn't see him go. One moment he was here, the next . . .'

He seemed to click back to the present, and looked from Art to Jonny and back again. 'Looking for something in particular?' he asked again.

'We saw one of your clocks the other day,' Art said. He thought it would be rude just to leave. 'A grandfather clock.'

The man nodded. 'I have made many grandfather clocks.'

'In fact,' Art said with a forced laugh, 'it belonged to the grandfather of the man who now owns it. So he said. I expect your father or grand-father made it.'

'Which clock was it?' He asked, Art thought, as a man might ask which of his children you had met.

'It belongs to a Mr Bartlett,' Jonny told him. 'Mr Roderick Bartlett.'

'1855,' the clock man said at once. 'Roderick Bartlett bought it in 1855. I recall him well. A thin-faced man. Very tall. *Long-case*, I remember I thought.'

'Well, his grandson owns it now. He's also called Roderick,' Art said. 'You ready, Jonny? We should get back to Flinch.'

'His grandson?' the clock man said quietly. He was shaking his head. 'I doubt it.'

Art and Jonny were at the door now. Art paused to say thank you to the man before they left. But as he turned, the clock man spoke again.

'I remember him well. 1855,' he repeated. He was looking down at the counter. 'A long-case man.' He looked up, his eyes meeting Art's. 'With a birthmark on his forehead, just here.' He tapped the left side of his bald head. 'Shaped like a star.'

Dad was interested to hear about Sladden and his paintings over dinner. He had cooked them pasta and some sort of sauce, though he was a bit vague about what exactly was in it. Arthur suspected this was because he did not want to have to admit it had come out of a tin and he hadn't read the ingredients.

Arthur briefly described his trip to the gallery and how he and Sarah had seen Sladden with the clock hidden in a cupboard. He thought Dad would have been interested to hear about his own clock, and how it had been spinning backwards. But neither Arthur nor Sarah wanted to mention it, and anyway it had stopped again after a minute or so.

'Can't say I noticed that picture,' Dad admitted. 'I probably didn't pay much attention to it. More interested in the ships. That Malcolm Brown was explaining about how you can tell different sorts of sailing ship.'

'Really?' Arthur tried to sound interested in this. He did not manage.

Sarah related how she and Arthur had met

Sladden on the beach the previous day. 'He's so clever. I don't know how he does it, but his paintings seem so dynamic. As if you're really there.'

'Like that one in the lighthouse,' Arthur remembered. 'Where it's like you're actually on the ship as it hits the rocks and breaks up.'

'The *Kairos*,' Sarah said.

'Is it? How do you know?'

'They all are,' she said simply. 'All his pictures are of the same ship. Haven't you noticed?'

'Well, if that's the case,' Arthur's dad said, 'they're not very accurate.'

'I bet they are,' Arthur countered. 'Sladden told us that he gets everything exactly right.' He turned to Sarah for support. 'What was it he said? About how if it isn't accurate it's a lie? Remember?'

She nodded. 'Something like that, wasn't it?'

'Well,' Dad said, 'I know you won't be impressed, but as a newly qualified expert in sailing vessels, I can tell you he's got it wrong. He isn't the only one, mind. Malcolm was telling me that traditionally the *Kairos* is represented as a sailing ship from the mid- to late eighteenth century – that model, for example up in the lamp room, that's based on a schooner. Or something.'

'Expert?' Arthur teased.

'Well, he did go on a bit and I forget the detail. But he was saying that by 1843, when the *Kairos* was wrecked, it would more likely have been a clipper. And that's ... different.'

'So Sladden got it wrong?' Arthur asked.

'Maybe it was an old ship?' Sarah suggested.

'Not according to the legend. Or so Malcolm says.'

Arthur felt disappointed, though he was not really sure why. 'Well,' he said, poking at his pasta, 'he must have got it wrong after all.' But he couldn't help feeling that there was more to it than they yet knew.

Chapter 8

They did not see Meg at all that Saturday. She did not come to the den, but Art was not worried. Not yet.

The next day – Sunday – they did not see her either. It was unusual for Meg not to come to the den on Saturday, but it did occasionally happen. But for her not to come on a Sunday either, if only for a few minutes to explain she was busy, was unheard of. By the time Art returned in the early afternoon, having shared lunch with his father, who was having a rare day off from Scotland Yard, he was quite anxious.

Charlie – Lord Fotherington, an old friend of the Cannoniers – turned up at the den at tea time and persuaded the three of them along to the Cannon Street station café. They did not need much coaxing, but without Meg, and with all of them now worrying even more about what had happened to her, it was a quiet and almost sombre session. It put Art in mind of the tea they had taken at Bartlett's house a few days previously – when Meg had seemed so happy. This did not help his mood.

Charlie knew they worked for the Invisible Detective, but he believed such a person actually existed. He asked what Brandon Lake was currently investigating, and what the Cannoniers were doing to help. Jonny made a game effort to explain about the mysterious – if it was mysterious – death of Mr Mason and how his brother thought his pocket watch was somehow to blame. Flinch mentioned the ghosts in the den, but even her enthusiasm seemed to be at its lowest ebb. Charlie could tell they were distracted, of course, but he did his best to hide it, for which Art was grateful.

'So, where's Meg?' Charlie asked at last.

Perhaps the inevitable question was prompted by Flinch's uncharacteristic refusal of a teacake. Or perhaps Charlie had just decided they'd avoided the question for too long.

Art looked at Jonny. Jonny looked down at the table. Flinch burst into tears and buried her face in her hands.

'Perhaps she's ill,' Charlie suggested, when Art stammered that they had not seen her, that they were becoming increasingly worried. 'There's a lot of flu around, you know.'

As soon as the words were spoken, Art felt as

if a heavy hand had been lifted from his shoulder. That must be the answer. It was so obvious.

'Have you asked her parents?'

'Her dad wouldn't know,' Flinch said quietly. Her face was streaked with drying tears, but she seemed to have been cheered by Charlie's suggestion. She pushed away her plate. 'I expect she's off her food.'

'We should take her something,' Jonny said. He looked away as if embarrassed by the notion. 'Flowers or something,' he added quietly. 'You know.'

'Well,' Charlie rose to his feet, 'I must be getting along. You give my very best wishes to Miss Meg, won't you. And if she is poorly, wish her a speedy recovery from me.'

'We will, 'Art promised. 'In fact, we'll go round to her house now and ask if there's anything we can do.' It would do no harm to talk to Meg's mother and set their minds at rest. After all, he thought, if she isn't actually ill, there must be a perfectly normal explanation for her continued absence.

But, for once, Art was wrong.

* * *

Meg's mother looked dreadful. She had dark rings under her eyes and her hair had not been brushed. She was rubbing her hands together, as if washing them thoroughly, while she stood in the doorway looking at Art, Jonny and Flinch.

'I'm sorry to disturb you on a Sunday, Mrs Wallace,' Art said politely. 'But we're friends of Meg's and we were worried about her.'

Mrs Wallace seemed to tense at this. 'Have you seen her?' she asked, her voice jangling with nervous energy and anxiety. 'Where is she? Is she all right? What's happened?'

'No – I . . .' Art had not expected this. He could sense Jonny and Flinch both watching him. 'We thought she must be ill. We haven't seen her for days. We were worried.'

'Who is it?' a gruff voice called from inside the house. 'Is that you, Margaret Wallace? If it is, you'll wish you'd never – ' The voice broke off as Meg's father appeared behind her mother and regarded Art and the others with evident suspicion and annoyance. 'What d'you want?' he demanded, swaying slightly as if caught in a breeze.

'We were asking after Meg,' Art said. 'We thought . . .'

But he got no further. The big man pushed past his wife and grabbed Art's lapels, almost lifting him off the ground. His breath stank of stale beer and old tobacco. 'If you know where she is, you'd best tell me right now,' he shouted, so loud that Art pulled away, blinking.

'Leave him alone,' Flinch shouted back. 'We ain't seen her, not for days.'

Reluctantly, Mr Wallace let go of Art and took a stumbling step backwards. 'If you do see her,' he said, jabbing his finger uncertainly in the air, 'you tell her.' He nodded, apparently convinced this was clear. 'Her mother's sick with worry. Missing for days on end.' He leaned towards his wife. 'These those friends she keeps going on about?'

Mrs Wallace shook her head. 'I don't know.'

'We *are* her friends,' Jonny insisted.

'We'll find Meg,' Art said, recovering from being shouted at. He wondered if Meg's parents had been to the police, but he suspected Mr Wallace preferred to steer well clear of 'the law'. Perhaps Art should ask his dad. 'We'll tell her how worried you are, Mrs Wallace. I'm sure she's fine,' he said, but in fact he was far from sure of that.

Mrs Wallace forced a smile. 'Thank you,' she breathed.

'You tell her,' Meg's father said again. Then he staggered back inside the house.

Meg's mother lingered a moment longer on the step, then she too went back inside. She paused before she shut the door, her eyes fixed on Art. They were like Meg's eyes – deep and full of emotion. 'Please find her. Tell her I – '

A large hand pushed the door roughly shut on her words.

They walked slowly along the street, heads down. Art felt drained and empty. He wished they had not come, but he also knew that they were better off knowing the truth, however unpleasant it might be.

'I think she's run away,' Flinch said.

'Don't blame her.' Jonny kicked at a pebble on the pavement and sent it spinning into the road.

'I'll talk to Dad,' Art decided. 'He can check the missing persons, have the bobbies keep an eye out for her.' But he did not really think that would help. Flinch was right – Meg had run away. 'But why?' he said out loud. 'Why's she run away from *us*?'

The cottage was draughty and cold. Arthur pulled the covers up to his neck and shivered inside. It must be midnight by now. He could not sleep. He had read for a while, until the print began to blur in front of his eyes. Then he had to get out of bed to turn the light off. Maybe after that he had dozed for a bit, perhaps he had slept. He wasn't sure.

One thing he was sure of, though. He wasn't getting out of bed again till morning. The storm had died down and the fog had rolled back in. It felt like the fog was there in the room with him, working its way into every nook and cranny, under the covers and into his pyjamas.

He turned over and closed his eyes tight, trying to shut out the cold. But it was no use. There was no bedside lamp, so if he wanted to read again he had to get out of bed and turn on the main light. And despite his previous certainty, Arthur threw back the covers and climbed out of bed. He paused by the window, wondering if the fog was thinning. He pulled back the curtain and looked out.

It was still misty, but the fog was nothing like as dense as it had been a few hours earlier. There was a strange stillness to the night, and the fog hung in the air in wisps and clung to the ground like small fallen clouds. It was like smoke creeping across the landscape, Arthur thought.

In the distance, swathed in the mist, he could see the dark shape of the church, the tower standing apart from the main structure as if afraid to venture closer. He could just make out the black smudges of gravestones, the faint line of the fence, the skeletons of the trees in the corner of the churchyard, clustered round the monument to the crew of the *Kairos*.

And something else. Movement. He leaned forward, almost bumping his nose against the cold glass. His breath misted it, adding to the swirling fog, and he wiped at the condensation with the sleeve of his pyjamas. There was no doubt about it – something was moving. Something besides the drifting fog. Figures, glimpsed only briefly through a gap in the mist, but figures he felt sure. Walking slowly through the churchyard towards the small wood.

* * *

'Where are you going?' she hissed.

Arthur had pulled on his trousers and a sweater over his pyjamas, socks and shoes. He was tiptoeing down the stairs when Sarah found him – her head poking round her bedroom door, her hair tangled across her face.

'For a walk,' he whispered back.

'Yeah. Right.' Her head disappeared, only to return a second later. 'Wait for me.' Then it was gone again.

Arthur continued down the stairs and waited in the hall. He'd give her two minutes, he decided, though he didn't have his watch on, so he'd have to guess when the time was up.

She was quicker than he expected, pulling a jumper over her head as she joined him. 'So what's the plan?'

'I want to see what's happening in the church-yard,' he told her. 'I thought I saw . . .' What had he seen? He wasn't really sure. Someone moving about maybe, but it was probably the rector locking up or something.

She didn't press him to explain. 'Let's go and see, then.'

They hardly spoke as they walked along the

path. Despite the fog, there was an almost full moon and so it was easy to see. Arthur led the way. When they reached the gate into the churchyard, he stopped and waited for Sarah. He put his finger to his lips. The moon had dipped behind a cloud, and the night was dark and shadowy.

'I thought I saw someone. Several people, in fact.'

She nodded impatiently and waved for him to lead the way into the churchyard.

They saw them almost at once. A ring of silent figures, standing motionless just inside the wooded area. Arthur counted them – seven. In a circle around the monument to the dead sailors.

'Who are they? What are they doing here?' Sarah murmured.

'I don't know. Some sort of ceremony, maybe.'

'It's close to the anniversary of the shipwreck, isn't it?'

'Let's get closer,' Arthur whispered.

She tugged at his sleeve. 'I don't like it.' She sounded nervous, which surprised Arthur. He thought *he* was the one who was nervous.

'It'll be all right. Just a little way, so we can see who it is.'

He would feel better once he had seen that it was just a few villagers keeping vigil. Besides, none of the silent figures could possibly know they were there, so long as they kept to the shadows.

He darted to the church tower, keeping close to the wall, conscious of Sarah right behind him. Although they were nearer, they could not see much more. Seven dark figures standing in a silent circle. But then, just for a few moments, the fog lifted, the moon came out again and the figures were illuminated in the pale light.

They were sailors. The men with their backs to Arthur were wearing dark jackets, stained and discoloured by the salt of the sea and ripped and worn through with age and use. But it was the men facing Arthur that made him gasp aloud. He heard Sarah too draw in her breath sharply.

They looked exactly as he imagined Long John Silver's crew must have looked in *Treasure Island* — with brass-buttoned jackets, thick belts with knives and flintlock pistols thrust in them, swords at their side. A huge earring caught the moonlight. Several of the men wore red headscarves, a couple had soft felt hats, others were bare-headed. One had an eyepatch.

The captain — Arthur *knew* it was the captain — was staring across the churchyard, straight at Arthur and Sarah. The moon was shining full on his face. Despite the hat, despite the pallid glow of the skull and crossbones, despite the way he stood beside his own monument, Arthur's attention was focused on the face. Apart from the black beard and the red scar running down the cheek, the captain's face was leached of colour. Just like the faces of the others standing around the monument to the shipwrecked sailors, it was drawn and pale and dead, the flesh hanging lifeless. Arthur was looking into the face of a man who had drowned 160 years ago. A pirate captain long since dead.

The pirate captain raised his hand, as if in greeting. Except Arthur could see that it wasn't a hand at all. The captain's sleeve ended in a barbed hook that was shaped like a cross between a machete and an old-fashioned pike.

The thunder rolled in again, the sky darkened and a ragged finger of lightning lit the dead figures like a camera-flash. Sarah grabbed Arthur's hand, dragging him away, back down the path. He staggered a few paces, unable to tear his gaze from the horrific figures. Then the spell was broken and he turned and ran with Sarah back to the safety of the cottage.

Chapter 9

'Meg's never missed a session before,' Jonny murmured to Flinch.

Usually, Flinch was bored by the Monday evening Invisible Detective consulting sessions. Usually, she stayed in the den or, if it was warm and sunny, sat on the steps outside and joined them after the session was over. But this evening she was concealed behind the curtain with Jonny.

It was a quiet meeting, subdued perhaps by the Invisible Detective's own rather downbeat mood. He was less expansive than usual, less amused at some of the more frivolous questions. He had started by saying that he would give an opinion on Mr Mason's pocket watch the following week, as investigations were continuing. There was some mirth at this, and it turned out that in any case Mr Mason had not bothered to return for a verdict.

It was as the session was drawing to an end that the problems arose.

'I would like to know,' a voice called out from the back of the room, 'why the famous cockerel at the Tower of London has not been seen nor heard this past week.'

'I didn't know there was a cockerel at the Tower of London,' Jonny whispered to Flinch.

She shrugged. 'Maybe he's lying. Testing us.' It happened every few weeks that someone tried to catch out Brandon Lake with a trick question. 'Meg would know.'

Jonny knew she was right. Meg would be able to tell at once if the man was lying, if he was testing the detective. He reached for the fishing rod, wondering if he should send Art a note. But what should he say – 'This man may be lying'? Art could guess that. It would be no help. Jonny held his breath and waited for the reply.

The Invisible Detective cleared his throat. 'The famous cockerel at the Tower of London?'

Jonny hoped he sounded more confident to the rest of the audience, but he could hear the hesitation in the detective's voice.

'That's right.' The man putting the question, on the other hand, sounded very sure of himself. Maybe he was not lying after all.

'Has not been heard or seen for a week,' Art's disguised voice said.

'That's what I said. Why, though? That's what I want to know.'

'I believe that the famous cockerel is ill,' the Invisible Detective announced.

It sounded a bit feeble, even to Jonny. Flinch too was frowning, as if she was worried at the way Art was handling the question.

'A wasting disease, I gather,' the detective added.

There was a moment's silence, then it was broken by a loud guffaw of laughter. 'Oh, Mr Lake,' the voice from the back of the room called out between bellows of amusement. 'Oh, Mr Detective, *sir* – I've got you this time and no mistake.'

Jonny felt suddenly cold, as if the blood had drained from his body. A trick – a trap, and they had fallen right into it. He did not blame Art, it was down to them all. But this could be the end for the Invisible Detective. To lose face like this . . .

'The famous cockerel,' the detective's voice said, surprisingly loud and confident over the laughter than was now spreading through the audience as more and more people got the joke, 'the famous cockerel at the Tower of London has

123

not been seen or heard for a week as it is suffering from a wasting disease.'

'Famous cockerel at the Tower!' someone shouted out, their voice collapsing into fits of hysterics.

'Oh dear, oh me,' someone else remarked close to the curtain.

Jonny could make out the faint shape of a man wiping his eyes and shaking his head.

'A wasting disease so severe,' the detective continued undeterred, 'that it has wasted away completely.'

The laughter seemed to hesitate at this.

'Because there is no such creature, sir. It does not exist.'

The amusement died.

The man who had asked the question continued to laugh for a few moments after everyone else had stopped. 'What is it?' he asked finally. 'Got him fair and square, didn't I?'

'I rather think he got you, Benny Jenkins,' another voice said. Jonny recognised it as belonging to Albert Norris, the landlord of the Dog and Goose. 'Fancy thinking Mr Lake'd be taken in by a story like that.'

Jonny breathed out heavily. 'Thank you, Mr Norris,' he murmured. He grinned at Flinch, and she grabbed his hand and squeezed it, grinning back.

'After that amusing little interlude,' the Invisible Detective was saying, with what sounded to Jonny like relief, 'I think it is time to draw our session to a close for this evening.' There was some shuffling of feet, and people began to make their way towards the stairs at the back of the room. 'Perhaps next week Mr Jenkins will be able to amuse us with more stories of non-existent and fanciful creatures from his overworked imagination,' the detective called after them.

There was more laughter at this. Jonny could hear people in the street outside calling out after the unfortunate Benny Jenkins as they left.

'You suffering from that wasting disease that's doing the rounds, Benny?'

'Maybe it's your brain that's wasting.'

'You shut up, Josh,' Benny called back, annoyed. 'Or I'll waste you. I was just giving him a chance to show his deductive powers.'

'Reckon its Benny's sense of humour that's wasted away,' someone else called.

But the voices and the laughter were fading into the distance now.

Art, Jonny and Flinch stood at the back of the room a few minutes later.

'That was close,' Jonny said. 'You did well to get out of that.'

'Skin of my teeth,' Art admitted. 'They gave me the benefit of the doubt this time, mainly thanks to Albert Norris. Won't be so easy next time.'

'Next time?' Flinch asked.

'There'll be a next time,' Art told her. 'The cockerel story was pretty obvious, looking back, but next time it might not be. And without Meg to tell us when people are lying, we'll get caught out. When we do . . .' He turned away.

'It'll be the end of the Invisible Detective,' Jonny finished the thought.

'We need Meg back,' Flinch said.

Art nodded. His face was drawn and pale when he turned round. 'We do need Meg back. But more important than that, we need to be sure she is safe and well.'

Jonny nodded. He was worried too. They all were. 'But where do we start?'

'I've been thinking about that. Why should Meg disappear *now*? What's happened this week that's unusual?'

'Something to do with her dad?' Jonny suggested.

Art shook his head. 'He wasn't very pleasant when we went round yesterday,' he admitted. 'But I think he was worried about her. And she's always had . . . problems with her dad.'

'That Bartlett man,' Flinch said. 'I don't like him.'

Jonny nodded. Actually, he had been thinking the same. 'That was weird, tea and those pictures and everything.'

'And the clock shop,' Art said. 'That's the other place we've been this week that may be important.'

'So what's the plan?'

'We keep watch. Whenever we're free. Flinch, you don't like Bartlett, and I agree there's something weird there. So you keep watch on the shop. Jonny will help you when he's not at school.'

'Right,' Jonny agreed.

Flinch was beaming – happy to have a job to do, and probably glad it didn't involve Bartlett.

'I'll keep an eye on Bartlett,' Art told them. 'To be honest, I can't see how either can be involved in Meg's running off, if that's what's happened. But Bartlett worries me. His interest in Meg, those pictures, and now . . .'

'That birthmark too . . .' Jonny said no more.

Art had wanted to tell Meg about it, to warn her that there was more to Bartlett than met the eye. But they had not seen her since.

'Yes. Of course, it may not be important or significant,' Art said. 'But these are the only clues we have.'

The motion of the boat was soothing. Dad had arranged with one of the local fishermen to taken them out into the bay for a couple of hours in an old motorboat. The weather was in stark contrast to the previous day's – bright sunshine and a cloudless sky had replaced the fog and storms. But it was still incredibly cold, and Arthur was glad he was wearing a jersey and a heavy coat.

Sarah was huddled next to him, while Dad –

apparently oblivious to the cold – was chatting with the fisherman.

'It was just people dressed up,' Sarah said. 'It must have been. Some sort of ritual or ceremony. Crazy, but not *scary*.'

'You reckon?'

'What else?'

'Ghosts,' Arthur suggested. 'The shipwrecked sailors come back to their own monument and graves.'

'Yeah,' she said sarcastically. 'That's really likely.'

They sat in silence for a few minutes, watching the activity on the harbour as it shrank into the distance. There was a man walking two dogs that strained and struggled to escape their leads; a couple of fishermen sitting on the quay, mending and folding nets; a small boy throwing pebbles into the water while his mother and younger brother fed the seagulls bits of bread.

'Why?' Sarah asked.

'Why what?'

'Why would they come back? I mean, if they are ghosts – which they aren't – why come back now?'

Arthur did not know. 'It's close to the

anniversary of the wreck, like you said. Or maybe it's to do with my clock going backwards.'

'It's stopped now,' she pointed out. 'And anyway, something must have made the clock do that.'

'Perhaps they're always there. Every night.'

'Mmmm.' She did not sound convinced. 'Fancy-dress party, more like.'

When they were well out to sea, the fisherman – whose name was Jack – pointed out landmarks on the shore.

'Before the lighthouse, there were many ships wrecked on the rocks here,' he told them.

'So when was the lighthouse built?' Arthur's dad asked him.

'About 1850. Malcolm Brown'd tell you.'

'I bet,' Arthur said quietly.

'Why so late? If there were often shipwrecks?' Sarah wanted to know.

'Oh there was a beacon before that. On the headland where the lighthouse is now. That warned most ships away.'

'Not the *Kairos*,' Arthur said.

He could remember the picture of the ship

being broken on the rocks. The sailors tumbling overboard, the mast breaking, the waves smashing into the splintering hull . . . Looking back from the boat, he could appreciate how accurate Sladden's picture of the coastline was. Although it was merely a dark mass in the painting, his contours and cliffs exactly followed reality. There was the point where a short stretch of beach had been visible, that was the slight lump in the cliffs where they protruded further into the sea, and over there was where the blazing beacon had been. For all the good it was.

'Hang on,' he said out loud. 'That's not right.'

Dad was talking to the fisherman about when the lighthouse was decommissioned and how ships navigated today. But Sarah heard Arthur's words.

'What do you mean?'

'The coastline, look.' He pointed. 'It's exactly as Sladden painted it, see. You remember the picture from the ship as it breaks on the rocks.'

Sarah shrugged. 'He used photos, probably.' Arthur must have frowned at this, because she went on, 'You're wondering how he knew the shape of the coastline when he never goes out in a boat, is that it?'

'No.' He had not been thinking of that at all,

but it was a good point. 'No, I'm wondering why he got it so wrong.'

'But it looks exactly the same. OK, so the painting shows it at night, in a storm, just hints at the shape of the land.'

'And it shows the beacon fire – over there, on that bit of headland close to our cottage and the church.'

'Yes.' Sarah frowned now. 'Yes,' she said again, more slowly as she considered this. 'But Jack just said the beacon was where the lighthouse now is – on the other side of the bay.'

Arthur nodded. 'So either Mr Accurate Sladden got it wrong or Jack got it wrong. Both of which are unlikely. Surely Jack's right – they'd build the lighthouse as a replacement for the existing beacon. That makes sense. Or ...' His mind was racing now, working through the possibilities.

'Or? Or what?'

'That's it!' He grabbed her by the shoulders and turned her so she was facing the headland where the cottage was – where the beacon had been. 'They're *both* right. And that's why the sailors have come back. Don't you see?'

'You mean, the beacon was in the wrong place?

For some reason they lit the fire that night on the wrong bit of cliff?'

'Not for some reason. It wasn't an accident. They did it on purpose.'

Sarah's breath misted the cold air as she realised what he was saying. 'They wrecked the ship. The villagers deliberately drove it onto the rocks.'

'Yes, for the cargo. They probably didn't even know what it was carrying. The fact it was pirates' treasure was just luck. But they wrecked the ship – murdered the crew.'

'And now . . .' she said quietly, her face pale with the cold.

'And now the dead sailors have come back to the village that killed them. For revenge.'

Chapter 10

It was so cold that Flinch could see her breath. She sat on the doorstep of a house on the other side of the street from the clock shop and blew out streams of mist from her mouth. She experimented with pushing her jaw forwards and breathing up so it warmed her nose. She tried curling her lower lip in over her teeth and blowing air down so it tickled her neck. And she watched absolutely nothing happening at the clock shop.

Nobody came. Nobody went. All day.

'You look like a dragon,' Jonny told her when he arrived from school. He had his satchel with him, and he flopped down beside Flinch and opened it. He rummaged round inside, while Flinch watched with interest. Eventually Jonny pulled out an apple and handed it to her.

'All quiet?' he asked.

'Yes,' Flinch said, sending bits of apple flying in among the misty breath. She giggled.

'Is the shop open? Is the clock man in there?' Jonny wondered after an hour.

Flinch nodded. She had walked past and looked in through the window when she arrived that morning. The bald-headed man with his long, thin moustache had been standing at the counter, winding up a clock. He had glanced up as Flinch looked in, and smiled. She smiled back. He looked like a nice man, but she had not gone inside. She had not bothered to check again, but she would have seen him leave.

'He told us he lives over the shop,' Jonny said when Flinch recounted this. 'At least, I think that's what he said. It was all a bit weird. He seemed to be telling us what his grandad did some of the time. I think.'

'I like pirate stories,' Flinch said. 'Tell me again.'

So Jonny told her. It passed the time. When he had finished the story, Jonny played I-spy with Flinch. Art had suggested to Jonny and Meg some time ago that this was a good way of helping Flinch at least learn her letters. It was usually a source of frustration to Jonny, who could spell very well. But since they had so much time it was a way of keeping themselves occupied.

'Grass,' Flinch decided.

'Not G,' Jonny said, 'C.' He sounded it out. 'Like cat and curiosity.'

Flinch frowned. 'Canary,' she said.

Jonny looked round. 'Where?'

'Nowhere. I was just saying. It begins with C.'

'Yes, it does. But it isn't the answer.' Flinch looked disappointed, but Jonny was not sure he could have chosen anything more obvious. They were, after all, outside a *clock* shop.

'Bartlett,' Flinch said suddenly. She shuffled back into the doorway where they were sitting.

'C,' Jonny told her. 'C-c-c-c-c,' he sounded.

'No, over there.' Flinch pointed down the street – to where a figure was approaching.

It was a man, tall and lean, wearing a cape and a hat. He looked rather old-fashioned, Jonny thought. But there was no mistaking him – it was indeed Roderick Bartlett.

'I spy with my little eye something beginning with "R",' Flinch said quietly.

Jonny nodded. They were both pressed back into the doorway now. 'Roderick Bartlett.'

Flinch frowned. 'No,' she said, pointing. Following behind Bartlett, keeping to the shadows, was another, smaller figure. 'Art Drake.'

When Bartlett went into the clock shop, Art ran over to join them. 'I couldn't believe it,' he said, squeezing into the doorway beside Jonny and Flinch. 'Does anyone live here?' He nodded back at the house behind them.

'No one's been in or out,' Flinch told him. 'I've been here all day. No one comes or goes at all round here.'

'Yes, as we got nearer I noticed how we saw fewer and fewer people. At first I thought it was just coincidence Bartlett was heading this way. After all, he doesn't live that far away. Then, as we got closer . . .' He paused to look across at the shop. 'Well, there's obviously a connection here.'

'Let's hope it helps us find Meg,' Jonny said. 'Do you think . . .' He broke off, not sure he wanted to say it out loud, not with Flinch there too. 'Well, do you think he's kidnapped Meg?'

Art sighed. 'I've tried not to. But yes, it is a possibility. That was why I wanted to watch his house – to see if I could spot any sign of her.'

'Did you?'

Art shook is head. 'Nothing.'

'Meg would signal,' Flinch assured them. 'She'd find a way to let us know she was in trouble.'

'I hope so.' Art stood up. 'Right, I think it's

time we found out what's happening inside the shop, don't you?'

'How?' Jonny asked. 'I mean, we can hardly go in and ask.'

'Look through the window,' Flinch told him.

The sun was low in the sky, reflecting off the window of the shop. Art hoped that meant it would dazzle anyone who tried to look out from inside. But he managed to find a point on the pavement outside from where they could see into the shop. He had a view of Bartlett's back, but the clock man was hidden from sight.

It was obvious what was happening, and boringly predictable. Of course Bartlett knew about the clock shop, because his grandfather had bought a clock there. If it *was* his grandfather, a niggling voice said at the back of Art's mind. He could not help remembering what the clock man had said about the birthmark – were birthmarks inherited? Art did not think so . . .

Bartlett was buying a clock. It was a simple brass carriage clock. Art could see it standing on the counter as the sale was completed. The clock man was writing in his ledger – Art could see his hands scratching across the page as he wrote out the details. Then the hand holding the pen disappeared, returning to view a moment later without the pen as the clock man picked up the clock and gave it to Bartlett.

'Scarper!' Art said as Bartlett turned.

Art darted for the side of the shop, hoping to conceal himself in the next doorway. Flinch was ahead of him. Jonny – faster than anyone else Art had ever known – had already disappeared.

'What kept you?' Jonny asked, grinning, as Flinch and Art piled into the same hiding place.

Art peered out cautiously and saw Bartlett heading back the way he had come.

'I'll get after him,' Art told the others. 'See where he's taking that clock.'

'What do you want us to do?' Jonny asked.

'I want you to go and talk to the clock man. Find out what he knows about Bartlett, and see if you can discover who he's bought the clock for.'

'You don't think it's for himself?' Jonny wondered.

'He's got clocks,' Flinch pointed out. 'Not just that broken grandfather clock. There were lots of clocks in his house.'

'Maybe he wants another one.'

'Maybe he does,' Art agreed. 'But it might be useful to know. Right, I'd better get going. Good luck.'

Jonny decided to wait a few minutes, so the clock man did not suspect they had followed Bartlett. Having mentioned him at their previous meeting, it was sure to seem like a coincidence anyway.

In the event, when they summoned up the courage to enter the shop, they found it empty.

'Hello?' Jonny called. He did not really want to see the man, but he felt bad about being in his shop without him knowing.

Flinch seemed to have no such scruples and was already behind the counter. Jonny thought she was going to look at the sales ledger, which was still open on the counter top. But she seemed to be interested in the photograph on the wall. The photograph of the clock shop.

'He's gone,' Flinch said, her eyes wide, as she turned back to face Jonny.

'I can see that.'

Jonny leaned over the counter so he could make out the latest entry in the ledger. The ink was darker than the others, newer. He shivered as he read it, and felt the bottom of his stomach tighten in fear and surprise. He hardly heard what Flinch was saying as she came round to join him.

'No, I mean he's gone from the picture. The clock man was in it, but now it's just a picture of the empty shop. Look.'

Jonny looked. For a moment he thought he saw the photograph. For a moment he thought Flinch was right and it showed a view of the shop – but with no clock man. A different picture. Then the picture disappeared, and Jonny realised that there was someone standing in front of it, blocking his view. As if he had just appeared there.

'Looking for something in particular?' the clock man asked, making them both jump with surprise.

'No,' Jonny stammered. 'No, thank you. Just . . . browsing.' He took Flinch's arm and pulled her with him towards the door. 'We were just leaving.'

'What is it?' Flinch asked as soon as they were outside. 'What's wrong, Jonny?'

'We have to find Art,' Jonny said. He was aware that he was out of breath, as if he had run for miles and miles. 'The new entry in the sales ledger – Bartlett's clock.'

'What about it?'

'It says the owner is Margaret Wallace.'

The mist was back, drifting close to the church and making wreaths round the gravestones.

'I still think it's people mucking about in fancy dress,' Sarah hissed as they crept along the path. 'They're probably not even there tonight.'

But they were.

The seven figures were standing as if they had not moved from the previous night, though Arthur knew they had not been there in daylight. But there was something different about them now. The men were swaying gently, as if in the breeze. As Arthur and Sarah sheltered in the angle of the church tower, the dead men began to sway more, shuffling their feet with apparent impatience. Slowly, they began to move – a step forwards, then backwards. Finally, as if at a command, they all turned in the same direction – towards their captain.

He raised his hooked 'hand', just as he had the previous night. Then he turned and started across the churchyard – towards where Arthur and Sarah were hiding. As he passed them, his men followed, until a line of shuffling dead shipwrecked mariners was making towards the church tower. Their pale, bloodless faces seemed to glow in the moonlight.

'I don't care if it's fancy dress or not,' Arthur said. 'It's time we left.' Taking Sarah by the hand, he ran for the gate on the far side of the church.

They had only got as far as the front of the church when Sarah pulled Arthur into the church porch.

'What?' he demanded.

'I don't think they're following us. Look.'

Arthur did, and saw that she was right. The pirates were staying on the path. They were making for the gate out of the churchyard, where Arthur had been heading, but they made no effort to change direction and follow Sarah and Arthur when they ducked off the path.

'So where are they going?' Arthur wondered.

'Down to the village perhaps. If you're right and they want some sort of revenge.'

'Then why didn't they just go there first? Why come up here?'

'Visiting relatives?' Sarah suggested. 'Bringing flowers for their own graves?'

But Arthur thought he knew the answer. 'Or maybe they didn't come here. Maybe this is where they have been all the time. I mean, if they're ghosts or whatever, they'd sort of rise from their graves, I suppose, wouldn't they?'

'They look pretty solid for ghosts.'

She was right again. The pirate captain was pushing the churchyard gate open with his hook, striding through and out along the path down to the village. The line of figures was silhouetted against the full moon as it started along the sloping cobbled street that led down to the harbour.

'What do we do now?' Sarah asked.

'Follow them.'

The mist seemed to cling to the pirates, shrouding them in a blurred halo. They walked at a steady pace, neither slow nor fast, but with a purposeful, deliberate tread.

Arthur and Sarah followed at what they hoped was a safe distance. The pirates did not seem to know they were there, but Arthur was ready to turn and run at any moment. He had no idea what to do for the best, other than follow and see what happened. He had thought of running back to the cottage – waking his dad, ringing the local police ... But he was pretty sure than neither of them would believe a couple of teenagers who claimed to have seen ghost pirates standing in a churchyard.

Once in the village, maybe other people would see them. It was nearly one in the morning, but perhaps there were still people leaving the pub, or a policeman on patrol, or the man walking his dogs ...

But there was no one. Not a living soul in sight – just the dead pirates making their way along the narrow cobbled street.

It took Arthur a while to realise they must know where they were going. They were heading in a definite direction, and it was not for the harbour, as he had assumed. They turned into a back street, and Arthur recognised it at once.

'They're heading for Sladden's studio,' he told Sarah.

'It'll be closed. That'll disappoint them.' She seemed to get even more sarcastic when she was frightened.

'But he lives there.' They hurried after the misty figures. 'Do you think they want to destroy his pictures or something? You know, wipe out all records?'

Sarah did not answer. She had paused at another corner and was watching the line of figures ahead of them. 'You're right. Look.'

The pirates were grouped round the entrance to the studio. Their captain tried the door, but it was obviously locked. He pushed and rattled the handle, but to no effect. Then he lifted his great hooked hand and smashed it into the wood. The door splintered, his hook stuck deep in it. He yanked it free and smashed it back in again, sending jagged fragments flying. The sound echoed round the street and off the cobbles, but no lights came on, nobody looked out of their windows, no curtains even twitched.

The captain stood back, and two of his men put their shoulders to the shattered door, forcing it inwards. It crashed down and they stepped through.

'Like you said, they're not ghosts,' Arthur murmured.

They ran to the studio, hesitantly peering round the broken doorframe. Three of the pirates were standing inside. The others must have gone on into the rooms beyond. There was a sudden roar of anger from somewhere above and Arthur could hear the rapid, heavy tread of someone descending the stairs in a hurry.

From elsewhere came the sound of a door slamming. Moments later, they heard the slap of feet on the cobbles. A figure appeared further up the road, running. Sladden.

'He got out the back door. Must have seen them coming,' Arthur said.

'Come on!' Sarah pushed Arthur ahead of her, away from the door.

A moment later the first of the pirates emerged from the studio. It paused for a second, head raised as if sniffing the air. Then it turned its blood-drained face towards Arthur and Sarah, and took a lurching step towards them.

They ran. Without really knowing where they were aiming for, they ran along street after street. Arthur tried to follow Sladden. He seemed to be heading out of the village, and together they must stand a better chance against the pirates. But from behind them they could always hear the heavy footfalls of their pursuers, while ahead they caught only fleeting glimpses of Sladden.

The road started to curl, and it was sloping upwards. Arthur was too out of breath to breathe a sigh of relief, but they must be back on the road up to the church and the cottage. The church might offer sanctuary of some sort; the cottage was where they could get help from Dad.

He looked back and saw the distinctive silhouette of the pirate captain emerging from the shadows of one of the last houses in the village. His hook was raised and in his other hand he held a cutlass. Dark shapes clustered impatiently behind him, following inexorably in Arthur and Sarah's wake . . .

Only when they reached the top of the incline and the road narrowed still further did Arthur realise his mistake. They were not on the way back to the cottage at all. They had taken the other road out of the village. Ahead of them, stark and tall in the moonlight, was the lighthouse.

Since there was no other shelter, nowhere else to hide, they ran towards it.

'There must be a phone,' Sarah gasped.

'If it isn't locked.'

The door opened at once, which surprised Arthur. He tumbled inside, with Sarah close behind him. As soon as he was on his feet he slammed the door shut behind them. There was no key in the lock, no bolts. Instead, he dragged the table over in front of the door, sending guidebooks and leaflets flying.

Then he turned to run up the stairs.

Sarah screamed as a figure loomed out of the darkness. Arthur grabbed her and they clung together, waiting for the cutlass to slice through the air towards them.

But the figure did not move. It stood watching them, immobile, as if amused.

Arthur laughed. It was a nervous sound rather than humorous. He reached out and prodded the figure on the chest. The lighthouse keeper rocked slightly on its stand, before settling back into its pose.

'Come on. Let's hide. I don't think they'll come in after us, but better safe than sorry.'

'Why don't you think they'll come in after us?' Sarah asked, her voice taut with nerves.

'I don't know. They haven't been interested in us until just now. Perhaps they'll move on somewhere else.'

They started up the stairs. Below them, the

tables scraped across the floor as the door was forced open. It jammed on the rough surface, one leg braced against the edge of a flagstone. A thin slice of moonlight cut through the gap between the door and its frame. Then it was blotted out by the shape of the large figure that was trying to force its way into the lighthouse.

'Arthur Drake!' The voice echoed round the tower. 'Arthur Drake – I know you are in there.'

Chapter 11

Art was surprised to see Jonny and Flinch. He listened carefully to what Jonny had to say, nodding grimly.

'He must be keeping Meg in the house.'

'Should we get the police?' Flinch wondered. 'Your dad?'

'They need proof before they raid someone's house. Not just our suspicions and the fact Bartlett has bought Meg a clock. It could be a present for next time he sees her.'

'It isn't,' Jonny said.

'*We* know that,' Art told him. 'But could you convince my dad? Or Charlie even? And if Bartlett sees policemen hanging around watching him or calling to ask him questions, he could hurt Meg. Or anything. No, the problem we have is how to get proof.'

'We go in and rescue Meg,' Flinch told them.

'Nice idea,' Jonny agreed. 'But it might be a bit more tricky than that. We don't know where he's keeping her. It may not be in the house at all. Could be anywhere.'

'We have to start somewhere,' Art said. 'The

problem is, we can't just turn up and demand to see Meg, and it would be difficult to pretend we've invited ourselves for tea again.'

'That creepy butler will be around some-where,' Jonny said. 'And I bet they keep the doors locked and bolted. Especially when they have prisoners.'

'So how do we get in?' Art wondered out loud.

'Through a window,' Flinch said.

'What, we just try them all in the hope we can find an open window and nobody notices?'

Flinch looked at Jonny as if he was mad. 'There's a window into a room where nobody ever goes. It's round the side of the house,' she said. 'I'll show you if you like.'

'Maybe there is,' Art said gently. 'You told us about the room. But I don't really want to go breaking windows.'

'You don't have to,' Flinch said. 'It's not locked. I know. I unlocked it.'

'Are you sure this is the same room?' Art was peering through the window that Flinch had led them to. 'The curtains are open.'

Flinch and Jonny were looking through as

well. Flinch had her nose pressed to the cold glass in an effort to see as much as possible. It was the same room – with the needlework on the chair, the book on the table, the carafe . . .

'Someone's cleaned it,' she said. 'And opened the curtains.'

'So they could come back at any moment,' Jonny said, taking a step backwards.

'Well, we have to take some risks,' Art pointed out. He pushed at the window, but it did not budge. 'You sure this is the one, Flinch?'

'Sure.'

'They probably locked it again when they cleaned the room,' Jonny said, still hanging back nervously.

'Maybe.' Art was still straining. 'I thought I felt it give a little then. Here, Jonny, give me a hand, will you?'

With both of them pushing, and Flinch helping as much as she could, the window slowly slid upwards. It opened a few inches, then jammed.

'Wiggle it,' Flinch suggested.

They did, coaxing the casement back and forth, first one end and then the other. After some effort, the two boys managed to force the window open a few more inches. Then a few more. Before long the gap was wide enough for Flinch to squeeze through.

Once Flinch was helping from inside the room, the window opened more easily, and soon all three of the them were standing by the table.

'We'll leave the window open,' Art said, 'in case we need an escape route.'

'I doubt we could get it closed again anyway,' Jonny added.

But Flinch was barely listening. 'Look,' she said, pointing across the room.

Under the portrait by the door there was a low cabinet with glass-fronted doors. Inside various ornaments and pieces of china were arranged. On top of it, centred below the portrait of the woman who looked like Meg's mother, was a clock. A brass carriage clock.

'That's it,' Jonny gasped. 'That's the clock he bought just now.'

'Look at the hands,' Flinch said.

They were moving. Not the slow, usual movement of the minute hand that you could only just make out if you watched carefully for long enough. The minute hand was moving like the second hand on a pocket watch. Even the hour hand was visibly making its way round the dial.

'How odd,' Art murmured.

'It's new as well,' Jonny said.

But before they could comment further, there was a sound from outside. The handle of the door began to turn.

'Quick!' Flinch gasped.

She looked round for a hiding place, but there wasn't one. And whoever came in would see at once that the window was open.

'Behind the curtains,' Art ordered.

They ran quickly and quietly back to the window and Art pulled the curtains in front of them as the door started to open. Dust swirled round them as they hid between the curtain and the open window. Art was peeping out through the gap between the two curtains, and Flinch crouched down to look out from below Art's vantage point.

It was Bartlett. He did not seem to have noticed anything was amiss and turned to examine the clock. He picked it up – probably, Flinch thought, because he saw it was broken. He had his back to her as he examined the clock, but Flinch thought she could hear the winding of a key. Then he replaced the clock on top of the cabinet and, after a quick glance round the room, he left. The door clicked shut behind him.

Almost immediately the clock began to chime. Flinch counted – six o'clock. That was about the right time, she thought.

Art opened the curtains and went over to the cabinet. 'Extraordinary,' he said. 'It's telling the right time and ticking properly. The hands aren't spinning round any more.'

'He's fixed it,' Jonny said.

Art picked up the clock, turning it over in his hand to examine the back. 'Look at this.' He held it out for them to see.

Flinch looked. It was writing, she knew that. But she could not read what it said. It was just swirls and curls to her. 'What's it say?'

'It says "Edax Rerum" on the front, on the dial,' Jonny told her. 'That's the name of the clock shop.'

'But this,' Art tapped the inscription engraved on the back of the clock. 'This says "Margaret Wallace".'

Flinch took the clock from Art and looked at

it. He must be right, but why did Bartlett want a clock with Meg's name on it? She was going to ask Art what he thought, but at that moment the door opened again.

This time there was no chance to hide. Flinch put the clock back on the cabinet and tuned to face Bartlett. Only it wasn't him. It was a woman.

It was the woman in the portrait above the clock. Or at least, it was a young woman who looked very like her. She seemed to be in her early twenties, slim and tall. Her hair was a mass of red curls that framed her face. She looked at the three of them in surprise.

'Flinch?' she said.

And although she had not recognised the woman, Flinch knew the voice almost as well as she knew her own.

'Meg?' she gasped. 'Meg, what's happened to you?'

Arthur paused on the stairs as he heard the voice echoing round the inside of the lighthouse.

'How do they know your name?' Sarah gasped.

'I don't know.' There was something familiar about the voice, but it was distorted by the reverberation and the distance. They were at the first of the rooms now, and Arthur ducked inside. 'Let's wait and see who it is.'

'The pirates.'

He shook his head. 'I'm not so sure.'

They stood in the shadow of the bunk beds against the wall, watching the staircase through the open door. A shadow fell across the doorway, broken and misshapen by the stairs. A figure had paused there, looking round as if unsure whether to continue up the stairs or look in the room.

'Arthur?' the figure called.

He almost laughed. 'Dad?'

'There you are. I saw you two come in here. What do you think you're playing at?' Arthur's dad strode into the room. He did not sound happy. 'When I saw you weren't in your bed, I thought you'd gone downstairs to get a drink or something. Instead I find you gallivanting round the countryside at the dead of night, taking Sarah with you.'

'I'm sorry, Mr Drake,' Sarah said, a little sheepishly.

158

'There are weird things happening, Dad,' Arthur tried to explain.

'You're telling me. I looked out of the window and saw you two heading into the village in the middle of the night . . .'

'But didn't you see who we were following?'

'Following?' He shook his head. 'It's time we got you home. I'm surprised this place is open.'

'We didn't break in, if that's what you mean.'

But Arthur's further protestations were cut short by the sounds from outside – heavy boots on the stairs.

'The pirates!' Sarah ran to the door and looked down the stairs. 'They're coming! Quick!'

Arthur's dad stared at them in evident bemusement. 'Is this some sort of game? You're supposed to get more sensible as you get older. More responsible.' He followed Arthur back to the door. Then he too heard the sound of approaching footsteps. 'That's probably Malcolm Brown, come to see what's going on in his precious lighthouse,' he told Arthur.

'No, Dad!' Arthur tried to catch his father's arm.

But it was too late. Dad had stepped out on the staircase.

Arthur and Sarah hurried after him. They found

him standing just outside the door, staring in dis-belief into the face of the pirate captain.

'Run!' Arthur shouted.

But his father seemed rooted to the spot. The captain gave an angry roar and thrust the man aside. Arthur watched as his dad tried to grab the pirate's arm, saw his dad's expression of bewilderment as he found he was wrestling with a hook rather than a hand. Then the pirate roared again and hurled Arthur's dad away from him. Dad went flying back into the room, tripping over the legs of the bunk bed and crashing to the ground. His head thudded into the floor, he groaned, and was still.

Arthur stared in horror and disbelief at his father's motionless body. But Sarah grabbed his arm and yanked him after her, up the stairs.

'Come on.'

'We can't just leave Dad to them,' Arthur protested.

'It's not him they want,' she shouted back, still pulling.

Arthur saw that she was right – the pirates were continuing up the stairs, ignoring the room and the unconscious man inside. Following Arthur and Sarah up the lighthouse.

Before long they were out of breath, but the pirates kept coming, following them up the stairs.

'Could we hide in one of the rooms?' Sarah suggested. She grabbed Arthur's arm as a thought occurred to her. 'What about the radio room or whatever it is? There's a telegraph thingy in there.'

'I doubt it's connected to anything,' Arthur said, pulling her on up the winding stairs. 'And even if it is, I can't work it. Jonny might have been able to,' he added quietly.

'Who?'

'Never mind,' Arthur muttered. 'No, let's keep going. We'd just be trapped in there.'

'We'll be trapped anyway when we reach the top.'

'At least the lamp room is glassed in,' Arthur said. 'Maybe we can get out there, or signal for help, or something. There's a gallery round the outside,' he remembered.

'Yeah, 100 metres or more above the ground.'

But she didn't have a better plan, so they kept running until they emerged into the lamp room. The moonlight shone in, making it light enough to see clearly. The first thing that Arthur saw was that Sarah was right – there was no way they could escape from here. The lighthouse towered high above the ground, and he doubted if anyone would be able to see them waving or hear them shouting from the gallery. Even if they were looking.

The second thing he saw was a figure standing, waiting for them. As they came in, he took a step backwards, almost tripping over his feet in fright.

'Keep away – you keep away from me, Jim Graves,' he shouted. He was holding something, a bundle wrapped in an oilskin, thrust out in front of him like a talisman to ward off the evil.

'It's only us,' Sarah said. 'Don't be frightened, Mr Sladden.'

'Not . . . not the pirates?' His voice was quiet, tired and almost pathetic.

'No,' Arthur told him. 'But they're right behind us.' He slammed the door shut and looked round for something to barricade it with. 'We have to keep them out of here until help comes.'

'Help?' Sladden said. He seemed almost in tears. 'There is no help.'

'We have to try,' Arthur told him. With Sarah's help, he managed to drag a display table across the door. 'Let's see if we can wedge it shut with some of those display stands and stuff.'

They had barely started to build a barricade when the door rocked under a tremendous impact from outside. Sladden gave a cry of terror and dropped to his knees. The oilskin bundle fell to the floor and something rolled out. The clock. The glass across the dial was cracked, the signs of the zodiac and the sun and moon hands distorted behind the fractured glass.

Seconds later, the door shuddered again. But this time something came through. The wood splintered along the grain, to allow a hard metal edge to appear. It was the tip of a sharp, curled spike. The pirate captain's hook.

Chapter 12

Meg stared in dismay and disbelief at her three friends.

'What are you doing here?'

They were looking at her in amazement. Well, that was hardly surprising, given how she had changed. It had amazed her too, when Roderick Bartlett had told her what he could do – had promised her a way of escape. She was sad at leaving her mother, but Mum would understand. In a few days when it was all sorted out and everything was properly arranged, Mum would understand. Perhaps she could even come and live with the two of them in this big house. . .

Then she had seen in the mirror, just a few minutes ago, what had happened to her. She had stood looking in disbelief at herself – just as Art and Jonny and Flinch were looking at her now.

'You can't stay,' she said sadly. 'You'll ruin everything.'

'Meg, what's going on?' Art asked.

He did not understand. How could any of them understand – they were just children. And even as she thought this, Meg began to realise what she had left behind, what she had decided to give up.

'Art,' she said, 'I'm sorry. I – ' Meg was not really sure what she wanted to say, except that suddenly, seeing her friends, seeing their reaction to her, she felt empty and disappointed and lonely. That wasn't how she was supposed to feel. Not like this.

She saw Flinch's eyes widen a moment before she felt a hand on her shoulder.

'What's going on?' Bartlett demanded. 'Did you invite these children in here, Margaret?'

'No,' she said. 'But –' But they are my friends, she was going to say.

He was not listening. Bartlett moved Meg gently aside and stepped into the room. 'How dare you?' he roared.

'We came to see Meg,' Flinch said defiantly.

The curtains on the other side of the room were blowing gently, as if in a breeze, and he strode over and thrust them aside. Behind, the window was open. When Bartlett turned back, his eyes were blazing. 'You force your way uninvited into my house and now you accost my fiancée.'

'Your what?' Art said. His expression was almost comical.

'Meg?' Jonny asked.

She nodded, turned away. 'Mr Bartlett – Roderick – has asked me to marry him,' she said quietly.

'Marry him?' Art laughed. 'Meg, you're not yet fifteen.'

'She is twenty-three,' Bartlett snapped. 'Not that it is any of your business.' He came over to Meg and took her hand. 'Whoever you think she might be, you have mistaken her for someone else. Someone who no longer exists. Margaret has agreed to consider my proposal of marriage and that is that. Nobody – but nobody – will interfere with my future happiness.'

Meg shuddered. He was right, of course – he had to be right. She had been so sure when he spoke to her. He was so certain, so convincing. So kind and gentle and thoughtful. He had offered her a way out, an escape – a life that sounded so much better than her own. But now Roderick Bartlett sounded more like her father when he ordered her mother around. 'Nobody', Meg suddenly felt sure, included herself. It certainly included her friends.

'Out, all of you,' Bartlett ordered. 'Now.'

'It's the clock, isn't it?' Art blurted as the three children filed into the corridor. 'You've done something to her with the clock.'

Bartlett froze, just as he was turning to follow them out. 'Nonsense,' he snapped. 'Don't be ridiculous.'

But Art seemed sure he was right. 'That's why the hands were spinning faster. Speeding up time. Now they've slowed again to their normal pace because Meg's already older.'

Meg was watching Bartlett closely, wondering what he would say, how he would react. His eyes narrowed almost to slits and his face seemed to darken. He was about to speak.

'No!' Meg exclaimed. 'Roderick – let them go.' She did not know what he was going to say, what he had decided to do, but she was frightened by that look, by his sudden fury. 'You've got me, that's what you want. Let them go.'

Bartlett watched her closely for a moment. Then he nodded. 'Very well,' he said, his voice dangerously quiet. 'But I would like a few words with them first about the propriety of breaking into people's homes.' He looked past Meg and raised his voice. 'Ah, Crow.'

Meg turned round. The butler was standing in the corridor on the other side of Art, Jonny and Flinch. He was holding a revolver.

'I heard a disturbance, sir,' he wheezed. 'Shall I contact the local constabulary?'

'Thank you, that will not be necessary. Show these people into the drawing room, if you would be so kind. And wait with them there until I have seen Margaret to her room.'

Crow motioned with the gun and, hands in the air, Art and the others moved along the corridor. As they went, first Art, then Jonny and finally Flinch turned and looked back at Meg. Art seemed sad. Jonny was angry. Flinch just shook her head as her face crumpled and tears welled up in her eyes. Then she turned and almost ran after the others, Crow following her. With the gun.

'You are so like her, you know.' Bartlett's voice was soft in Meg's ear. 'So very like her.'

'Your first wife?' He had explained that she reminded him of his first wife – had shown her the pictures. He said her name was Katherine. It was a nice name. Meg had a great-aunt called

Katherine, her mother had mentioned her. But she was long dead.

'You won't hurt them, will you?' she asked, almost afraid to put the question.

'Of course not.' He took her hand and led her back to the stairs. 'They'll come to no harm at all. I'll just give them a good dressing-down and make sure you never have to see them again.'

Meg nodded. She allowed herself to be led up to her room. When Bartlett – she was no longer thinking of him as Roderick, she realised – when he had first told her what he could do, first asked her if she would agree, Meg had been impressed by his self-confidence and honesty. She could tell that he really could do what he promised. That he really did care for her. That he really did want what was best.

But now she knew that his ideals and hers were very far apart. It was not just that, seeing Art and the others, she suddenly realised how wrong she had been and how much she missed them, though that was a part of it. 'Of course not,' he had said. 'They'll come to no harm at all.' He had smiled reassuringly as he said it. Patted her hand gently to show his sincerity. But Meg knew, just as

169

she always knew. She hadn't grown out of it, she thought, with a mixture of relief and disappointment. She could still tell without any shadow of doubt that Bartlett was lying, and that her best friends – the people she cared for most in the whole world alongside her mother – were at that moment in the most terrible danger.

The door was giving way under the pirate captain's onslaught. Blow after blow sent splinters and fragments of wood flying across the room. One caught Arthur on the cheek, stinging and drawing blood.

'What do they want?' Sarah asked. She was cowering behind a display screen, close to the model of the *Kairos*. 'Why do they want *us*?'

Sladden was kneeling on the floor, cradling the clock in his arms and rocking back and forth, whimpering. Arthur watched him, moving like a pendulum to a regular rhythm. And with every movement, another piece of the puzzle clicked into place.

'They aren't after us, Sarah. They were never after us. They're after him.' Arthur pointed at Sladden, who looked up at Arthur's words. 'Aren't they? That's the whole point of this, isn't it? You called him by name – Jim Graves. Captain James Graves of the *Kairos*.' A whole section of the door came free and somersaulted through the air, close to where Arthur was standing. 'That wasn't a guess, was it – you knew who it was. Just as he knows you.'

Sarah was looking from Arthur to Sladden. 'But how can he know? Unless . . .' Her eyes widened at the thought. 'That's impossible.'

'Is it? You paint everything so accurately, you said,' he told Sladden. He was having to shout now above the hammering at the remains of the door. The makeshift barricade was lurching under the repeated impacts. 'Yet you knew exactly how the wreck of the *Kairos* would look from the ship. You knew where the beacon really was, not where it was supposed to be. How could that be? Unless . . .' He paused as the barricade shifted forward. One of the pirates was leaning through the hole in the door, pushing pieces away, trying to force his way into the room.

'Unless I was there,' Sladden said. He had

171

stopped rocking and was staring up at Arthur. 'You're right. I was on that ship.'

'And the experience was so terrifying, you vowed never to go to sea again.'

He nodded.

'But how?' Sarah shouted. She grabbed Arthur and pulled him back from the barricade as a cutlass carved through the air and bit into one of the display stands. 'How is it possible?'

'The clock,' Arthur told her. 'That's how. That's why he had it hidden away in the cupboard. And somehow that's what's brought the rest of the crew back.'

'The captain got it in the Far East. An island off the coast of Penang. Won it at cards from an old man who said his life had already stretched on for longer than he cared to remember. It was just a clock then, of course. But the old man, he tinkered with it for Graves. And the captain insisted he make it over to the ship rather than just to him. He engraved the name of the ship on the back of the clock. *Kairos*.' Sladden gave a short, humourless laugh. He was staring at the disintegrating barricade. 'Time . . .'

'Then the villagers wrecked the ship,' Sarah

said. 'The rest of the crew was killed, but you escaped.'

The display stands and tables lurched again. One of the stands toppled forwards and crashed to the floor. The broken remains of the door were forced open a few more inches ...

'The water was so cold.' He was staring into nothingness, eyes glassy and salt-wet. 'I thought I would never surface. I kicked and kicked, but I couldn't let go of the clock.' He hugged it to him tightly as he remembered. 'I had to keep hold of the clock.' He looked up at Arthur. 'That was everything. Don't you understand?'

The last remains of the barricade scattered across the floor.

'So long as I had the clock I was safe.'

The final surviving sections of the door collapsed to the ground.

'Safe from the sea.'

The first of the pirates lurched into the room and stood waiting.

'Safe from the wreckers.'

One by one, the drowned crew of the *Kairos* stepped over the broken barricade and grouped in a semicircle round Sladden, Sarah and Arthur.

'Safe from *him*.'

And James Graves, dead captain of the wrecked *Kairos*, stepped into the semicircle and turned his pearl-like eyes towards Arthur and the others.

Chapter 13

The hunched butler, Crow, kept them at gunpoint in the drawing room where a few days earlier he had served them tea.

Art, Jonny and Flinch sat together squeezed onto the chaise longue, and Crow stood in front of them, watching them through his little eyes. His head was angled in concentration, so that he did indeed look like a malevolent crow. The gun never wavered.

They sat there for what seemed like ages before Bartlett entered the room. He looked at Art, Jonny and Flinch, but none of them said anything. Then he turned to Crow.

'Miss Margaret is resting in her room,' he said quietly to the butler. But Art could hear, 'I do not wish her to be disturbed by the sound of shots, unless absolutely necessary.'

Crow nodded his understanding. 'Sir,' he muttered.

Bartlett looked back at the three of them. 'So wait half an hour, until she is asleep.'

'And then what?' Art asked defiantly.

Bartlett looked at Art, his eyes burning with

hatred. But when he spoke his voice was level and calm, his words intended for Crow. 'Then shoot them,' he said.

Meg had told Bartlett she was going to get some sleep. She had yawned and stretched and made a show of laying out her nightdress. But as soon as he was gone, she had tiptoed to the door and listened. When she was sure she could hear nothing outside, she eased it open and looked cautiously out on to the landing.

Her room was near the top of the stairs and she could just hear someone talking in the distance, their voice floating up from below. Bartlett, she was sure – the voice was strong and rich. She leaned over the banisters and strained to hear.

'Then shoot them.'

The words were faint but clear. There was no way she had misheard them. Meg stood frozen for several seconds as she tried to decide what to do. Then she heard footsteps in the hall below, the soft tread of someone starting up the stairs, and she ran back to her room, hoping desperately she would not be heard.

Once in the room, she rushed to the bed and bundled her nightdress under the covers. Then she climbed in after it, pulling the sheets up to her neck. She turned her head away from the door so that, if he looked in, Bartlett would not see her face – would not see the anger and fear she knew it would betray.

The door opened. Meg heard the handle turn and the slight squeak of the hinges. She held her breath. It seemed like she held her breath for ever, but at last there was another squeak and the click of the door closing again. Had he left?

Meg sighed, trying to make it sound like she was stirring in her sleep. She turned over, again hoping it seemed she was still asleep, and opened her eyes just enough to peep out.

He was still there – standing just inside the room with his back to the door. Watching her. It was all Meg could do not to cry out in surprise and fear. Bartlett did not move, and after a minute Meg wondered if he intended to stand there, watching her, until he heard the gunshots from downstairs and knew that her friends were dead. How long did she have? How long before Crow put a bullet in each of the children? She admired

Art more than anyone, had complete confidence in his ability and intelligence. But even Art couldn't stop a bullet.

Children. She had thought of them as *children*. Yet she didn't really feel any older now than she had before she 'grew up'. Inside, she was the same. Yet her body had skipped forwards years. She had missed so much, she began to realise – the friendship of Art and the others, the joy of growing up *together* . . .

After what seemed an age, Bartlett took a step forwards, and again Meg almost cried out. But then he turned, opened the door and left. The door closed quietly behind him.

At once Meg was out of bed and across the room. She almost tripped over her feet on the way – she was still not used to being taller, to her longer legs, bigger feet. She had expected that increasing in size, changing shape so rapidly, *growing up*, would solve so much. That it would leave her elegant and independent. But instead it had made her clumsy and a prisoner. She caught her balance and hoped she had made no noise.

The landing was deserted. Meg thought – hoped? – she could make out the sound of footsteps from along the corridor that led to Bartlett's study. He could spend hours in there, she knew. Which would give her time to rescue the others. Somehow. But how?

She had reached the bottom of the stairs before an idea occurred to her. In an alcove close to the drawing-room door stood the grandfather clock that she had first come here to ask Bartlett about. The drawing-room door was open, so she was careful to be as quiet as possible.

The hands were set at twenty past seven. There was a narrow gap between the clock and the side of the alcove, just wide enough for Meg to squeeze into. Flinch would have no trouble at all, she thought, with a sad smile. In fact, Flinch could have hidden in the gap behind the clock – between the clock and the back wall.

'You can't shoot us,' Meg heard Art saying. 'It's murder.' He sounded nervous. Desperate.

Meg knew she did not have long. She cupped her hands round her mouth and shouted, making her voice as low as possible: 'Crow!'

'Sir?' The reply sounded very close. If he came out of the drawing room into the hall and heard her calling from the alcove, she was done for.

But she had to risk it. 'Crow,' she called again. 'Come here. Leave those brats and get along here at once.' She had to admit that her voice was well disguised. But she also had to admit that she did not think it sounded anything at all like Bartlett.

'Sir?' Crow called again. 'Sir, but – Where are you, sir?'

'Just come here. Now.' She tried to sound impatient and angry. Was that the sound of footsteps?

'Don't you even think about leaving this room,' she heard Crow say.

She held her breath – he sounded like he was right by the alcove. If he walked past, he would probably see her. She had hoped he would go the other way – down towards the library and the kitchens. But what if Bartlett had told him he was going to his study? What if he went past the alcove and upstairs?

What, Meg thought with a sudden rush of fear, if Bartlett had also heard her calling? He might be running from his study at this moment . . .

A dark figure stepped in front of the alcove, hesitated, seemed to realise there was someone hiding there – and turned.

But it was not Crow. 'Oh, Art – thank goodness.' Meg almost hugged him. But somehow he looked so small and vulnerable. She was not used to looking down at him.

'Meg – was that you calling?'

She nodded. Jonny and Flinch had appeared beside Art. Jonny looked shaken, but Flinch was grinning.

'You have to get away,' Meg said. 'Quickly, before he comes back.'

'You're coming too,' Art said.

She shook her head. 'No.'

'But why?' Jonny asked.

'You can't stay here,' Flinch told her.

'I have to. Don't you see? Not just to keep an eye on Bartlett, but because . . .' She sighed. 'Because only Bartlett can make me young again, turn back the clock.'

'Is that what you want?' Art asked gently.

'Yes,' she said. It was almost a sob. 'Go on – quickly.'

Somewhere in the distance she heard Crow calling out. They all turned towards the sound.

'The clock man,' Art said. 'He might be able to help.' Art took Meg's hands in his own and

181

looked up at her. 'We'll be back soon. We'll be back for you,' he promised.

By the time Meg had blinked away the tears, the front door had closed behind them and they were gone. She sniffed, wiped her eyes on the back of her hand and ran back up the stairs.

Of course, Jonny reached the clock shop first – well ahead of Art and Flinch. When they arrived, he was standing outside, kicking his feet nervously.

'It's shut,' he explained. 'Locked up.'

'I could climb in the window again,' Flinch offered.

'That's no good,' Jonny told her. 'We need to see the clock man. He isn't here.'

'But he lives above the shop,' Art remembered.

'So? It's shut.'

'So,' Art said, 'remember the old sea captain?'

Jonny nodded. 'He hammered on his door with his hook.'

As Flinch pointed out, they did not have a hook. But the three of them banged and thumped on the shop door for all they were worth. It seemed as though they kept it up for ages, certainly until Art's fists were raw and bruised.

'It's no good,' he admitted at last. 'He must be out. Let's face it,' he went on glumly, 'I doubt he could have helped us anyway.'

'Looking for something in particular?'

The words made Art jump in surprise. He had not heard the door open, but the clock man was standing there, regarding the three children suspiciously.

'Er, yes,' Art said. 'I'm sorry to disturb you after you've closed for the evening.'

The clock man shrugged and stepped aside to let them troop into the shop. 'The clocks don't stop just because it is getting late,' he said.

'We have a friend, Meg, who's in trouble,' Art explained. 'I think perhaps you can help us.'

The clock man's attention flicked from one of them to the other, like a pendulum swinging back and forth. 'Help you?'

'Someone bought a clock for her,' Jonny said. 'From here.'

'This *is* a clock shop.'

'I have a pocket watch too,' Jonny said. He

held out the watch that Mason had left for the Invisible Detective. The watch that had first got them involved in looking for the shop.

The clock man took it and examined it. 'The owner of this watch,' he said slowly, 'died.' He turned it over and showed the plain back – the smooth surface where the name had been engraved only a few days previously. Now there was no sign of it. 'Tell me about your friend,' he said as he handed it back to Jonny.

'Her name's Meg,' Flinch told him. 'And she's got older.'

'A man bought her a clock,' Jonny added. 'Bartlett. You remember?'

The clock man nodded. 'Indeed I do.'

'Can you help us?' Art asked.

The clock man seemed to consider. Then he said, 'No.'

Their disappointment was almost tangible. It seemed to hang in the air like a cloud.

'But,' the clock man said, with the vaguest hint of a smile, 'you can help yourselves. That pocket watch might also help. That and the clocks that Bartlett already has in his possession.' He was standing behind the counter and now he leaned forwards, his hands on the surface. 'It is all a matter of balance, you see. For every clock that goes too fast, there is another that goes too slow. That pocket watch had a partner – as you know from my sales ledger.' He was definitely smiling now, and Art swallowed, feeling suddenly guilty. 'The only clock I know of that was not one of a pair was the captain's. But I am sure that somewhere, somewhen, it had a brother.'

This all seemed nonsense to Art, but Jonny was nodding enthusiastically. 'Bartlett,' he blurted out, 'he's the original Bartlett, not the grandfather, isn't he? And his clock – it's a slow clock. That's why it doesn't seem to be moving but the time does change. Only very slowly.'

It was as if someone had switched a light on. Suddenly Art could see what the clock man was saying. 'Meg's clock was going fast,' he said. 'Then it went back to normal speed.'

The clock man nodded, as if to a bright pupil. 'Your friend got older,' he said. 'Then her time returned to normal.'

'So we can turn back Meg's clock?' Flinch said. She was frowning as she tried to work it all out.

But the clock man shook his head. 'Sadly, each clock can either go fast or go slow. But the mechanism does not allow for both.'

'So Meg is stuck as she is,' Art realised. The thought made him feel pale inside.

'I am afraid so.' He straightened up and looked at Jonny. 'That watch you have. It stopped when the owner died, though even then there would be some strange effects, perhaps. Time is forever playing tricks on us.'

Art nodded, remembering the 'ghosts' in the den.

'After all, the energy it draws and gives to its partner must go and come from somewhere. But currently it has no owner. There is no name engraved on the back.' He opened a drawer at the side of the counter and rummaged through the contents. 'But your friend's clock will have her name on it, just as Bartlett's will have his. While the clocks are theirs, they are influenced by them.' He had found what he wanted in the drawer and held it out to Art. It looked like a pencil, but made of metal.

Art took it, examined it. It was like a small screwdriver, he thought, only the tip was a sharp blade. 'What is this?'

'Your friend's clock is a fast clock, though now it beats the seconds in real time. Bartlett has a slow clock, and you – ' he pointed at Jonny – 'are holding a fast watch. One holds back or rewinds. The other speeds up or jumps ahead. I trust you now understand the distinction.' The clock man reached out again and gently tapped the handle of the tool he had given to Art. 'This is an engraving tool,' he said. 'I think you may find it useful. But,' he said slowly, fixing Art with a piercing look, 'remember that possession is nine points of the law, and think carefully before you use it.' The clock man straightened up again. 'Now, if you will excuse me, I think I shall need to arrange for a collection and a delivery.' There was a twinkle in his canny eyes. 'The readiness is all, as they say.'

'You're dead, Jim Graves.' Sladden was shivering as he stared up at his former captain. 'You've been dead 160 years.'

The pirate captain stood towering over Sladden. When he spoke, it was a harsh, grating sound, like the sea raking back over heavy shingle. 'Is it really that long?'

Arthur and Sarah were behind Sladden, pressed back against the display case with its model of the *Kairos*. 'What do you want?' Arthur said, trying to keep his voice from shaking.

The captain did not move. He was staring down at Sladden. 'What is mine. What is ours. What you stole, Martin Sladden.'

'The ship was wrecked, you were dead.' Sladden shuffled backwards.

'If we were dying, it was because you took the clock.'

Sladden dragged himself to his feet and stood facing his captain. He was shorter than Graves and shaking with emotion and fear. 'Dying? *You* were going to kill *me*.' He turned to Arthur and Sarah. 'They were going to make me walk the plank.'

'Murderer,' Captain Graves hissed.

'Murderer,' the other pirates echoed.

'It was an accident,' Sladden pleaded. 'A fight. He came at me.'

'You killed Robin Fisher. Stabbed him. Through the heart.'

'Through the heart,' the pirates whispered.

'My first mate, and you stabbed him. For his share of the treasure.'

'It wasn't like that.' Sladden turned to Arthur, his eyes wide and desperate. 'Tell them.'

Arthur shook his head, opened his hands. He did not know what to say. 'I wasn't there. I don't know.'

'You were tried by your fellows and found guilty,' the captain said. He took a step forwards.

Sladden cowered away. 'I found him taking the treasure, helping himself to the gemstones.' Another step backwards.

'Guilty,' the pirates intoned, as they stepped after him.

Captain Graves stopped. He looked down at the floor, a sudden snap of the head.

'No!' Realising what the captain was looking at, Sladden hurled himself forwards, tried to knock him away.

But two of the pirates stepped forwards, surprisingly fast, grabbed his arms and dragged him back. Sladden was held helpless, spread-eagled, watching as the captain bent slowly down and picked up the clock. He looked for a moment into the cracked dial, then back at Sladden.

'He wanted more than his fair share.' Sladden's

voice was almost a whimper. His whole attention was on the clock, watching as the pirate captain slowly turned it over. 'You have to be fair. You have to be accurate. Otherwise it's just a lie.'

The pirates were all watching their captain. 'Just a lie,' they breathed. The words seemed to hang in the air.

Arthur moved sideways so he could see what the captain was doing. He was conscious of Sarah close beside him, clutching his arm. She was shaking, and Arthur knew that he was shaking just as much. The fog seemed to have seeped into the lighthouse. The air was misting and swirling.

'You scored out our name,' the captain said. He turned the clock so Sladden could see the back of it. There was a deep, savage groove carved into the metal. Below it was scratched, in hesitant letters picked out with rust, 'Martin Sladden'. 'Betrayed your fellows. Sentenced us to a watery grave that should have been yours.'

'No.' Sladden was shaking his head, trying to break free of the two pirates, but they held him tight by the arms. 'No, it was the villagers. They wrecked the ship, lured us onto the rocks. It's them you want. It's them that killed you.'

The captain turned the clock away, angling it so he could see the defaced back-plate. 'They have been wrecking ships here for hundreds of years. They had as much right to trick us onto the rocks as we had to attack the merchantmen and raid the coastal ports. But you . . .' His stabbed his hook forwards, the brutal point close to Sladden's trembling face. 'You betrayed your crew. Your fellows. Your friends. You stole from *us*.' The captain nodded slowly. 'And we have come to reclaim what is ours.'

'No!' Sladden shouted, as if realising only now what the captain intended.

He struggled even more, managed to rip one arm free and lashed out. But another pirate stepped forwards, catching the man's arm and holding it.

'You can't!' Sladden looked across at Arthur and Sarah. 'Stop him, please. You must stop him.'

Captain Graves lowered his hook, resting it gently on the back of the clock. He held it so that Sladden – and Arthur and Sarah – could clearly see where the point of the hook was positioned beside Sladden's scratched name.

Then, with a sudden, vicious convulsion that seemed to ripple through the gathering mist, he dragged the sharp point of the hook savagely through the letters, obliterating them.

A thin peel of metal curled away from the back of the clock, detached itself and fell to the floor. Mirroring its fall, Sladden collapsed as his captors let go of his arms.

With deliberate but surprisingly fine strokes, the Captain scratched a new name in the back of the clock: 'Kairos'.

Sladden looked up. He stretched out his hand, as if to stop the captain, but it was too late. The face that looked up was lined and pale, wrinkled and old. The thinning hair had faded in a moment to grey, then white. The hand that stretched out was withered, skeletal, trembling bone. The man that fell forwards, collapsing as his ancient knees gave way, was already crumbling to dust. Dust that seemed to swirl and fade with the wisps of fog that drifted across the lamp-room floor.

The captain looked up from the clock. He did not seem to see the crumpled, empty clothing at his feet. He turned towards Arthur and Sarah.

'Go,' he whispered. 'Go now.'

Together they edged round the group of pale figures and stepped over the scattered remains of the barricade. They were almost at the door when Arthur felt the cold edge of the captain's hook descend on his shoulder.

'Not you,' the captain rasped. 'The girl can go. But you must stay here. With us.'

Sarah was ahead of Arthur. She turned and looked back at him, her eyes wide and full of fear.

When she spoke, her voice was trembling and tense. 'If he stays, we both stay,' she said.

Chapter 14

The window at the side of the house that gave into the room where they had found Meg's clock was still open.

'Lucky. I thought he'd close it after he found us in here,' Art said as he climbed through and into the room.

'He did.' The voice startled Art and he caught his foot on the sill, almost falling. 'But I opened it again. I guessed you'd try this way.'

Meg was sitting at the table, watching Jonny and Flinch climb in after Art. She set down the book she had been reading, marking her place with a ribbon. She looked at Art, her familiar yet so different eyes holding his. 'Can you do it?' she asked. 'Is it possible?'

'Meg,' he said, 'I really don't know. But I think so. If we understood what the clock man was saying, but . . .' He did not like to go on. He was not sure how to tell her that she might be stuck older for ever, or that if they tried to change things and got it wrong they might just make them worse.

Meg was shaking her head. 'Don't tell me the

"but". Let's just do it.' She stood up and went over to the brass carriage clock on the cabinet. 'Is this what you need?'

'We need to scratch your name off the back,' Jonny said.

Meg picked up the clock and handed it to Art. He pulled out the engraving tool and scratched through her name, watching her carefully. 'No ill-effects from that?'

She shrugged. 'Not as far as I know.'

'Now, we have to get the real Meg back,' Flinch said. 'That's what Art and Jonny think.'

'The real Meg?' She looked at them, her expression as unreadable as ever. 'Yes,' she said at last, with a sad smile. 'Yes, that's what we have to do.' She took the clock from Art and replaced it on the cabinet.

Art was relieved. He had wondered whether Meg actually wanted to get back to her real age. He was sure she wanted to get away from Bartlett, but being grown up – in so many ways, he suspected, that was what Meg had always wanted. 'We need Bartlett's clock. The grandfather clock in the hall. Is he . . .'

'In his study, I think, upstairs. And Crow is

sulking somewhere.' Meg's mouth twitched as she tried not to smile. 'He got a good dressing-down, as Bartlett calls it, after letting you escape. Don't worry, they didn't seem to realise I had anything to do with it. Crow thinks it was all Bartlett's fault. And Bartlett, of course, won't listen to him.'

The house seemed quiet and empty. They made their way through to the hallway without seeing or hearing any trace of Bartlett or Crow. Art drew the engraving tool out of his pocket and squeezed, with difficulty, into the alcove beside the clock. There was a gap between the back of the clock and the wall, but it was too small for him to get into, and too dark for him to see what he was doing if he just reached round behind the clock.

'We'll have to pull the clock out a bit further, maybe turn it,' he decided.

'I thought Flinch could fit behind,' Meg said.

'I could,' she agreed.

'And I'm sure she could scratch out Bartlett's name on the back,' Art said. 'But I don't think she could write your name, Meg.'

Flinch looked down at the ground, embarrassed and upset she could not do the job. 'Just cause I can't write.' She looked up hopefully. 'I could copy it, though. I know the letters. Most of them.'

Art smiled at her. 'It will only take a moment. Come on, Jonny, help me shift this.'

Together, with Meg helping and Flinch whispering helpfully, they angled the clock so that Art could get behind. Sure enough, engraved on the back in the same flowing, stylised script he had seen on the carriage clock, and on the pocket watch before it faded, was a name: 'Roderick Bartlett'. Art looked at it, holding the engraving tool poised, wondering if Bartlett might somehow know what was happening. He hoped he was doing the right thing.

Then he reached up and scratched the sharp point through the engraved name, scoring it out. Underneath, in handwriting he knew his teachers would tell him he should be ashamed of, he scratched 'Margaret Wallace'.

'Nothing's happened,' Flinch pointed out when Art reappeared from behind the clock.

'I was afraid of that,' he admitted. Art looked at Jonny. 'This is a slow clock, so Meg won't be getting any older, but Bartlett is now ageing at a normal rate.'

'So we just have to wait until Meg really should be the age she now seems, then we can scratch her name off the clock.'

Meg was aghast. 'You mean – I'm stuck like this?'

Art nodded, unable to think of anything to say. He and Jonny pushed the clock back into place.

'Unless . . .' Jonny said suddenly. He was at the clock now, examining the dial. As they watched, he swung open the glass door and reached for the hands of the clock. 'If Bartlett can make a fast clock go forwards, or stop . . . Er, tell me if this hurts or anything,' he said to Meg. Then he started to turn the hour hand backwards round the clock.

It was like watching a film wind backwards, Art thought. Meg seemed to shrink, to change shape. Her face seemed wider now, her eyes larger, her hair more abundant as her head shrank inside it . . . Her features softened, and he could see freckles fading into view on her cheeks and across the bridge of her nose.

'I think . . . Is it working?' Meg asked, watching Art and Flinch's reactions.

Jonny paused and looked round. 'Crikey, I'll say so.'

'Is that about right, do you reckon?' Art wondered. 'It looks like Meg to me, but maybe you should wind her back a little bit more, make her a bit younger? What do you think?' he asked Flinch.

'Go back more,' Flinch said. She grinned mischievously. 'Make her into a baby.'

'Don't you dare!' Meg snapped.

It was a tone that Art knew only too well. And with it he recognised perfectly the expression of sullen annoyance. 'No leave her like that,' he told Jonny. 'That's exactly right. That's the *real* Meg.'

'Now we have to get that carriage clock so Bartlett can't make her old again,' Jonny said.

'That's right.' Art handed the engraving tool to Flinch. 'Here, Flinch. You scratch Meg's name off the back of this clock, just in case. I know you can do that, and I didn't think to do it before we put the clock back. I'll never squeeze behind there now, but you can.'

Flinch grinned and took the sharp tool. 'I can do it,' she assured him. 'You get the clock and I'll catch you up.'

'Right.' Art led Jonny and Meg – the real

Meg – back down the corridor to the room where they had come in. 'Plain sailing now,' he said quietly. The door was still standing open, and Art grabbed the clock from the cabinet, turning in triumph to face his friends. 'We just need to get this clock away from here.'

'I'm afraid that will not be possible.' Roderick Bartlett was standing in the doorway, holding a gun. Beside him, the hunched butler Crow glared angrily at Art, Jonny and Meg.

It took Flinch only a few moments to score out the writing on the back of the clock. She could not read it, but she knew it said 'Margaret Wallace'. She could recognise her own name – even write it, though Art was forever telling her off for drawing a little circle above it where he said there should just be a dot.

Pleased with herself, she ran back down the corridor to the room where they had climbed in. But as she approached, she saw Bartlett and Crow in front of her, stepping into the doorway.

Her first thought was to run back the other way and let herself out through the front door. But she could hear Bartlett's rich voice and guessed from his smug tone that he had caught the others. She edged her way along the corridor and peered into the room.

Bartlett was standing with Crow just inside the door, and had a gun levelled at Art, Jonny and Meg. Flinch moved slightly so that Art could see her. He nodded slightly as he caught sight of her. He was holding the brass clock.

'Now, Crow,' Bartlett was saying, 'if you would be good enough to fetch a sharp knife, I shall engrave Miss Wallace's name on the back of the clock again and we shall be able to restore her to a sensible age.'

'I'm happy as I am,' Meg said angrily.

'Your happiness really does not come into this, my dear. Not any more.' Bartlett turned to his butler. 'Crow.'

'Sir.'

Flinch ducked to the side of the door and pressed herself hard against the wall as Crow shuffled out of the room. He headed off down the corridor, without seeing her, and Flinch breathed a sigh of relief. She moved back to the door.

'Now,' Bartlett said, 'give me the clock.'

Art was looking directly at Flinch as he

answered, watching her intently over Bartlett's shoulder. 'Here,' he said. 'Catch!'

The clock was past Bartlett before he could react. He scrabbled in the air, almost dropping the gun, but he was too late.

It took Flinch by surprise too, and she caught the clock awkwardly, because it was heavier than she had imagined. As soon as she felt it safe in her hands, she turned and ran. She knew that Bartlett would be after her in a moment – as soon as he realised what had happened. She needed somewhere to hide and she knew just the place.

Bartlett charged out of the room after Flinch. 'Leave that room and I'll shoot you,' he shouted at them as he went.

As soon as he was through the door, Jonny darted across the room. 'I've heard that before.'

'We can't leave Flinch,' Meg said.

'I'm not.' He stopped in front of the table and picked up the discarded sampler from the chair.

'Good idea,' Art said. 'He'll be back in a minute.'

'What are you doing?' Meg demanded. 'We don't have time for needlework.' She strode across the room and snatched the bundle of material from Jonny.

'I'm not doing needlework,' he said. 'Well, maybe I am.' He held up the needle he had pulled from the material. It was dull with rust and felt rough between his finger and thumb.

'You're going to stab him with a needle?'

'It's tempting,' Jonny admitted. Holding the needle carefully, he took out the pocket watch with his other hand.

'Flinch has taken one of his timepieces,' Art said quietly. 'It seems only fair to replace it.'

Jonny was having trouble making a mark on the back of the watch. The needle was old and blunt, and barely scratched the surface. He could feel it bending as he tried to score the downward line of an 'R'.

'Do you think initials would do?' Art asked, seeing the trouble he was having.

'Maybe. I hope so. It's all I can manage.' If Jonny angled the watch to the light he could make out the rough 'RB' he had scraped on the back. Would it do? He turned the watch over and all three of them crowded round it. The hands were not moving.

'Well, it was worth a try,' Art said, patting Jonny gently on the shoulder.

'And what have we here?' Bartlett was back. He looked flustered and red in the face.

'You didn't catch her, then,' Meg said.

'No matter. She can't escape. And I have you three as hostages to ensure she returns eventually.' He was looking at the watch that Jonny held, his eyes narrowing. 'Where did you get that?'

Nobody answered. Bartlett gave a short laugh. 'It will do you no good, in any case. Even if you were able to assign that watch to me, it would merely cancel out the clock in the hall. Oh, I know you have scratched my name off the back. But there is no other name on it now and the clock is still in my possession.'

'And possession,' Art said slowly, 'is nine points of the law.' He was looking at Jonny as he said it, his eyes wide and his expression serious. 'Remember?' he added quietly.

Jonny remembered. He was not sure what it meant, but he recalled the clock man's words.

'Ah, Crow.' Bartlett turned as the butler lurched into the room. He was holding a thin-bladed knife. 'Get after that girl. She has the clock.'

Crow held out the knife to Bartlett, but he shook his head. 'You may have more use for that than I, at the moment.'

As he spoke, Bartlett turned towards Crow for a moment, gesturing for him to leave. But a moment was all Jonny needed. In a flash he was across the room. Bartlett turned quickly and caught him by the arm, evidently thinking Jonny was trying to escape.

'Oh no, you don't,' he snarled, pushing Jonny back towards the others.

But he had missed what Meg and Art had both noticed. He had not seen what Jonny had done. He pointed the gun at the three children. 'Now,' he said, 'we shall wait and see what happens.'

Art and Meg both glanced at Jonny.

'We shall indeed,' Art said quietly.

Squeezed into her cramped hiding place, the carriage clock on the floor between her feet, Flinch strained to hear if anyone was nearby. She thought she could hear Crow shuffling past, but it might have been her imagination. She wriggled slightly, trying to get comfortable. Something was digging into her side and she thought it must be the engraving tool she had thrust into her pocket.

But it was not the tool. It was a small piece of thick card. She pulled it out and held it up so she could see the writing on it. She could not read what it said, but she realised that did not matter.

There was very little space behind the grandfather clock, but Flinch was able to wriggle about and get the engraving tool out of her pocket. There was just enough light from the hallway to see what she was doing now that her eyes had adjusted. Just.

The sound of the lorry was loud through the open window on the other side of the room. The engine idled for a moment, then cut out. Art could hear men shouting to each other, the clanking of chains and the crash of metal.

Bartlett had heard it too and, still keeping them covered with the gun, he crossed the room. He held the curtain back and leaned so he could see out of the window. At first he looked curious, then distracted. But after a few moments, the colour drained from his face and he almost dropped the gun.

With hardly a glance at Art and the others, he ran from the room.

'Crow!' Art heard him shouting urgently.

All three of them ran to the window to see what was outside, what Bartlett had seen. It was a lorry. A large lorry of the type used for deliveries or removals. Beside him, Jonny gasped and Art angled his head slightly so he could see what Jonny had seen.

The doorbell rang. But Art hardly heard it. He was staring at the name painted on the side of the lorry. Edax Rerum.

'The clock shop,' Meg murmured.

'No, Crow!' Bartlett's distant voice sounded weak, almost a croak. 'Don't answer the door!'

'Come on.' Art was running. He did not care whether Bartlett had a gun or not, he wanted to see what was happening.

The front door was already open. Two men in overalls were standing in the hallway. Crow was trying to usher them out again, but they ignored him.

'This is it,' one of the men said. 'This is the one.' They were standing in front of the grand-father clock.

'No!' The voice was little more than a wheeze. Only when he heard him, did Art realise that Bartlett was also in the hall. He was leaning on the wall, as if he could barely stand. He seemed somehow thinner, smaller. As he reached out to try to stop the two men lifting the clock, Art could see that his hand was wrinkled and curled, the fingers crooked with age.

'Excuse me, sir,' the second man said politely as they lifted the clock and moved it gently out of the alcove. 'Got to deliver this to its new owner.'

Bartlett took a stumbling step forwards. But his knees were bent and he seemed more stooped now than his butler. Crow stood watching helplessly, shaking with indecision and fear. As he fell, Bartlett turned, twisted. Art could see his face now – framed by thinning white hair, it was lined and discoloured. The wrinkles seemed to deepen even as Art watched.

Bartlett tried to drag himself after the removal men, hands clutching forwards, claw-like on the carpet, as he inched closer to the door. Closer. Every moment, he seemed to age and weaken.

Art followed him, horrified and yet fascinated. As he drew level with the alcove where the clock had been, he saw that Flinch was standing there. She looked as frightened and confused as Art felt. She was holding the engraving tool in one hand, a card in the other.

'What's happening, Art?'

'I don't know. What did you do?'

Bartlett was at the door. It seemed an effort for him to keep his head raised so he could see – so he could see the clock being loaded into the back of the lorry. Then the back was swung up, holding chains rattling, and the bolts were slid home.

He crawled forwards another few inches, then toppled over and fell down the steps. His hand was stretched out in a vain attempt to stop the men as they climbed into the front of the lorry.

'I scratched on the back of the clock,' Flinch said.

Meg took the card from her. 'It's Mr Jerrickson's business card.'

'I just copied his name. Scratched the letters.'

'Well done, Flinch,' Art said.

Jonny patted her on the back.

'He said he wanted a clock,' Flinch said. 'P'raps it'll do instead of the rent.'

As Roderick Bartlett's aged body fell forwards, his eyes wide and staring, the watch that Jonny had wound up and slipped into his jacket pocket fell out. It hit the bottom step, the glass over the dial shattering. The back sprang off and a mass of cogs and springs scattered across the step – rolling and bouncing away from Bartlett's trembling fingers.

The fingers convulsed one last time, then were still. His eyes closed. A breeze seemed to be blowing across the front of the house. As the lorry disappeared into the distance, the hand that was stretched out after it was pale, brittle bone . . .

'Just go,' Arthur told her. 'They won't harm me, I'm sure.'

In fact, he was far from sure, but he did not want Sarah to stay and suffer whatever fate the pirates had decided was due to him.

'I can't just leave you.'

'Please. Find Dad. Check he's all right and get back to the cottage.'

'You're sure?' She sounded relieved, looking from Arthur to the tall, silent pirate captain and back again. 'You'll be OK?'

'I'm sure. I'll see you back at the cottage soon. Promise.'

Sarah was biting her bottom lip as she considered. She nodded, looked as if she was about to say something else, but then simply turned and ran from the room. Arthur could hear her footsteps fast on the staircase.

When the sound had faded completely into the stillness, Arthur turned to face the pirate captain. 'What do you want?' he asked. He had expected to feel afraid, staring into the cold bloodless face of the drowned man. But he felt nothing. Just cold and numb and empty.

The captain was holding the clock. He brought it up in front of him, level with Arthur's face. 'It is broken,' he said quietly. 'The glass is cracked. The mechanism is damaged.'

'I'm sorry.' Arthur looked at the other pirates. They were grouped round him now, just as they had been round Sladden. 'It isn't my fault,' he said. But was it? Had he somehow distracted Sladden and made him knock the clock to the floor? Was that what this was about – punishment for breaking the clock?

'You have a clock.' The captain took a step towards Arthur. 'I know that you have a clock, like this one. It may have a different aspect, it may not show its true face on its dial. But you have a clock. I know this from your own aspect, from the fact that you are here. From that fact that *we* are here.'

'You want *my* clock?' he stammered. 'I don't have it here with me. It's at the cottage.'

But the captain was shaking his head. 'That clock is yours. You have your own purposes for it, I think.'

'Then what?'

'This clock must be repaired. I have some knowledge of how it works, some insight into the intricacies of the mechanism. But I am not capable of repairing the clock.' Another lurching step forwards. The grey face was thrust close to Arthur's. He could smell the salt and the decay.

'You want my help to repair the clock?'

The captain nodded. 'You must know of these things.'

'But I don't. I'm sorry.'

The captain's head sagged forwards. 'No hope ...' he whispered, so quietly that Arthur barely heard him.

'Unless . . .'

The head come slowly up again. 'Unless?'

Arthur swallowed, trying not to breathe in the smell. But could he remember from the Invisible Detective's casebook? 'There is a man.' He paused. This was not going to help. '*Was* a man,' he corrected himself. 'I don't know if he's still there, or rather if his shop is still there. It's a clock shop, you see. He repaired clocks. Like yours.'

'Where?'

'In London. I can't remember the name of the street, but the shop is called Edax Rerum.' He remembered what his grandad had told him. 'As in *Tempus edax rerum.*'

'Time devours everything,' the captain whispered. 'When is this shop?'

'When?' Arthur frowned. 'What do you mean, when?'

As if in answer, the captain held up the clock.

'It was certainly there in 1937. But I'm not sure how real it was then. But the clockmaker, he was there long before that.'

'Our ship was wrecked in 1843.'

'Yes,' Arthur agreed. '1843. I'm sure it was there in 1843. But – but that's 160 years ago.'

The mist was getting thicker. The figures of the pirates seemed to be fading into it, dissolving, becoming mist themselves.

'It is time for us to return,' the captain said to Arthur.

'Return? Where?'

'To where we belong.' He turned to look at his crew, standing behind him, then stepped past Arthur and towards the door. He paused in the doorway and looked back again. 'Thank you,' he said. Then he stepped out of the room and, one by one, his fading crew drifted after him. Like mist.

The door onto the gallery opened easily. Arthur stood outside the lamp room, looking down at the ground far below and taking in huge, deep breaths of fresh air. The night was clear and still, the landscape lit by the full moon.

In the small car park at the base of the lighthouse he could see the tiny figure of Sarah and, beside her, his father. Dad was rubbing his head and pacing up and down.

'Completely barmy.' Dad's voice drifted up to the gallery. 'Dressing up and parading round as pirates in the middle of the night. They're lucky someone wasn't badly hurt. Probably drunk and disorderly, if you ask me ...'

Arthur could not hear Sarah's response. He hoped she was agreeing with Dad, not telling him that the mad villagers in fancy dress were actually dead pirates wrecked off the coast in 1843 and returning for the last of their crew ...

He turned to go back inside. He had better join them. And he had better start thinking of a good reason why he and Sarah had been out at the lighthouse in the middle of the night. Perhaps they had seen the villagers and followed them. Was that believable? It was something close to the truth after all. But it also occurred to him that his father was more likely to believe that Arthur and Sarah had wanted to spend some time alone together. He felt his face redden as he wondered how close *that* was to the truth.

As he made to step back into the lamp room, Arthur caught sight of something else. In the distance, picked out in the moonlight and swathed with mist, was a sailing ship – a sailing ship that Arthur recognised all too well from Martin Sladden's paintings. And between the ship and the rocky shore, a tiny rowing boat was bobbing slowly towards the horizon. Mist seemed to pour out of the boat so that the detail was vague and nebulous. But Arthur could just discern the shapes of the six figures sitting in the boat, two of them pulling rhythmically at the oars – in, out … Like a pendulum keeping steady time.

At the front of the little boat, standing proud and looking out towards his ship, stood a seventh figure – Captain Graves. Silhouetted against the misty sea, he slowly turned. Arthur could imagine him lifting his pale eyes to look up at the lighthouse. As he watched, the pirate captain raised his hooked hand in farewell. Then he turned back towards the *Kairos*.

'Goodbye,' Arthur murmured.

But the mist was rolling in again and both the sailing ship and the rowing boat were gone.

Chapter 15

Jonny's well-practised flick of the fishing rod sent Meg's note through the air to the Invisible Detective.

'That is indeed intriguing,' the detective was saying.

Jonny could imagine Art taking the slip of paper from the fish hook and peering at it in the dim light.

'A door that, no matter how often it is bolted from the inside, is unbolted again in the morning. Since it is not a lock, we cannot assume someone else has a key. And you say there is nobody else in the house.'

'That's right, sir.' Jonny could hear the smugness in the man's voice now. How had he missed it before?

Meg glanced back at Jonny, hiding with her behind the curtains. She nodded, as if to say 'I told you so.' She had realised at once of course.

'Intriguing,' the detective repeated. 'Or rather, it would be . . . If there was a grain of truth in your story.'

Jonny was grinning at Meg. Beside him,

Flinch grinned too. And after a moment, Meg seemed to give in and the hint of a smile curled her lips.

On the other side of the curtain, the audience was murmuring. The man who had told the story about the bolted door protested, but he was shouted down and laughed at.

'Really, I tire of such petty attempts to test my ability. They succeed only in vexing my patience. And now,' Brandon Lake's voice cut into the hubbub, 'does anyone have a genuine question? I believe we have time for just one more this evening.'

'I have a question,' a voice said. It was a quiet voice, an old man's. It was a voice Jonny recognised though he could not place it.

Flinch pushed past Jonny and Meg and peered out between the curtains. 'It's Mr Jerrickson,' she whispered.

Art had recognised the voice too, because the detective replied, 'Yes, Mr Jerrickson, it is kind of you to join us for a change.'

'Just thought I'd see what goes on in my top room. And I do have a question for you, Mr Lake.'

'Go on.'

'It isn't to ask why I never see you, though I do wonder at that of course. No,' he went on, 'my question is this. Now, don't think I'm ungrateful, sir, but I just wonder where the very elegant grandfather clock that was delivered to me came from.'

There was a pause. The dimly lit room was silent for a moment before the Invisible Detective replied.

'The clock used to belong to a Mr Roderick Bartlett, but he has no further use for it. More than that I cannot tell you, except . . .' The detective hesitated before going on, 'Except that although the clock does not appear to keep time, it is indeed a very attractive and elegant timepiece and you would do well to keep it in your possession.'

'Thank you, sir,' Mr Jerrickson said. 'I think I shall take your advice.'

The session drew to a close and the people departed. Jonny could hear them chattering and gossiping as they left. Some were delighted that the story about the bolted door had been so easily rumbled. Others were impressed that the Invisible Detective could even tell the history of a grandfather clock without any apparent prior knowledge.

Jonny counted the money while Meg and

Flinch helped Art out of the huge coat. 'Another case closed,' Jonny said.

'Almost,' Art told him.

'What do you mean?' Meg wanted to know.

'Yes, we solved it all,' Flinch protested.

Art grinned at her. 'Yes, we did. Another triumph for the Invisible Detective, and we'll celebrate back at the den. I'll see you all back there soon.'

'Soon?' Meg asked. 'Why? Where are you going now?'

'Not far. I won't be long.' Art pulled on his jacket and straightened his tie. 'There's just something I want to do first, that's all.'

'Fine,' Jonny said before either of the girls could answer. He didn't know what Art was talking about. But he trusted Art more than anyone else in the world, and if Art wanted a few minutes to himself for whatever reason, then that was fine with him. 'We'll see you back at the den soon.'

Jonny led Meg and Flinch down the stairs and out onto Cannon Street. 'I'll give you both a head start,' he said. 'But the last one there's a dirty rascal.'

* * *

The road was as quiet and deserted as Art remembered. He saw no one from the moment he turned into Jursall Street until he left again.

The house was blank-faced and empty, the boarded and broken windows as he recalled. But it held no ghosts for him now. He was not surprised that the front door was unlocked and he pushed it open.

There was a smell of dust in the hallway – musty and decayed. The door to the steps down to the cellar was standing open. Holding on tight to what he was carrying, Art pulled his torch from his coat pocket and shone it down the stone steps. He knew that at any moment the whole cellar might be lit up and the house shake. But that did not worry him. He was more concerned about dropping the brass carriage clock.

It had taken him a while to decide what to do with it. Meg didn't want it. None of them did. But Art was not sure it was safe to destroy the thing, or even if it was possible. So he had decided to bring it here, where it could wait.

He chose the central alcove, from where he knew the concealed passageway led. Art could not help shivering as he remembered the adventure with the ghost soldiers that had started in this house. An adventure in which himself and Meg and Jonny and Flinch had all played their part, and from which they had been lucky to escape with their lives.

He placed the clock in the middle of the shelf at the back of the alcove. For no real reason at all, he adjusted the hands so they told the right time – ten minutes past seven. But he knew they would not move again for many years.

Happy with this, Art turned to leave. And found a figure standing behind him, at the bottom of the stairs. It was a boy, about his own age and size but dressed differently and wearing a cap. He was holding a clock. And as Art looked into the boy's surprised face, he thought it was like looking into a mirror.

'Hello, Art,' the boy said.

He was not sure why, but almost as soon as they were home again Arthur knew he had to go back to the old house on Jursall Street – the house where he had found the clock.

It was gone seven o'clock on the Sunday evening before he got there. Dad was working. He had remained convinced they had witnessed some weird village pageant down in Cornwall, and despite some stern words, he did not seem too annoyed that Arthur and Sarah had gone to watch the late-night festivities.

Sarah was back at home with her mum and her brother. But he would see her at school tomorrow. They had not really had much of a chance to talk since leaving the lighthouse. Arthur's dad had been with them most of the time and they were both exhausted after their adventures.

They had enjoyed a final meal at the pub the following day, before they headed back home. There had been some talk in the village about vandals causing trouble at the lighthouse, though Arthur had managed to make sure it didn't reach his dad's ears. He wondered how long it would be before Sladden was missed.

Only when Arthur made his way down to the cellar, pulling the clock from his rucksack and holding it in front of him as if to ward off the long-gone ghosts, did he realise why he had come here.

There was someone else in the cellar already.

A boy of about Arthur's own age was adjusting the hands of a clock which stood on the shelf at the back of the central alcove. There was something insubstantial about both the boy and the clock. As if they were not really there, but somehow made of smoke.

The boy turned, caught sight of Arthur and blinked in surprise.

'Hello, Art,' Arthur said. 'My name's Arthur Drake, and you won't believe this, but you're my grandad.'

Art turned and looked back towards the alcove.

'That's right,' Arthur told him. 'It's the clock. Somehow it's letting us talk like this. I don't know how long we have, but there's loads of things I want to ask you about.'

'Your grandad?' Art repeated. 'But – you're the same age as I am.'

'I am now. But you'll grow up. Get married. Have children.'

Art looked carefully at Arthur. He seemed to have trouble focusing on him, and Arthur guessed he must also seem insubstantial, like mist.

'*Tempus edax rerum*,' Art said quietly. 'You know,'

he went on, louder now, 'I have such strange dreams sometimes. I say the oddest things and see the strangest visions and I don't know why.' He nodded as if things were becoming clear at last. 'Yes,' he said, and grinned. 'There are loads of things to talk about.'

The sound of knocking was loud in the still of the moonless night. It echoed through the shop as the clock man made his nervous way to the door. He had been sound asleep a minute ago. All around him clocks clicked their way through the middle of the night.

He was a large man, silhouetted black against the dark grey of the outside, when the clock man opened the door. He had a hand raised, ready to knock again. Except that it was not a hand, but an iron hook.

The clock man stepped back into his shop and the figure followed him. Under its other arm it carried an oilskin-wrapped bundle.

'Looking for something in particular?' the clock man asked, his throat dry and nervous.

The figure held out the bundle it was carrying. There was a strange smell in the air – like you caught on the breeze down by the river when it was a warm day. But the night was cold and still.

The clock man took the oilskin and carefully pulled it away from the clock that was inside. It was a clock like none he had seen before. Instead of numerals, the dial was marked with the signs of the zodiac. Instead of hands, a sun and a moon orbited the dial. It was old. He could tell it was old. Such craftsmanship, he thought – it looked like it was made only yesterday.

The man who had handed him the clock was standing in the deepest of the shadows beside the door. But the clock man could begin to make out something of his features. A sailor, that was certain. He could not see the man's face, just the darker shadows of a beard, the shape of a cutlass at his side. When he spoke his voice was a dry rasp.

'The ship's clock,' he said. 'It has been dropped.'

'I have never seen anything like it,' the clock man confessed, his voice taut and nervous.

'Then look at it. Examine it. Copy it, if you can. That is your fee for mending it.'

And so the bargain was struck between the clock man and the pirate captain, on a cold, dark night in the February of 1843.